I closed my eyes and murmured the words that would let me access the cats' power. Within seconds I felt their feline life forces. Without thinking, I coiled my muscles. I crouched and jumped easily to the top of our seven-foot brick wall. I landed on my toes, arms out for balance, but felt solid and secure.

Laughing aloud, I raised my face to the sky. I saw differently, heard differently, tasted the air more powerfully. I smelled other animals, damp brick, green leaves and decaying plants and dirt. I was giddy with sensation, thrilled, with fierce anticipation about exploring the whole new world opened to me. My night vision was amazing, and I gazed at everything, seeing every dark leaf, every swaying plant, every cricket in the grass, one crisp, clear snapshot at a time.

I was super-Clio, bursting with life and power, and a dark and terrible joy rose up in me.

I sat down again in my circle, trying to still my frantically beating heart. I didn't *want* to lose this feeling, this incredible, exhilarating extra-ness. It would be so easy to just take it, take it and keep it, and not care about the consequences.

By Cate Tiernan

BALEFIRE

SWEEP

BALEFIRE

BOOK THREE
A FEATHER OF STONE

CATE TIERNAN

razOr
bill

Balefire 3: A Feather of Stone

RAZORBILL

Published by the Penguin Group
Penguin Young Readers Group
345 Hudson Street, New York, New York 10014, U.S.A.
Penguin Group (USA) Inc., 375 Hudson Street, New York, New York 10014, U.S.A.
Penguin Group (Canada), 90 Eglinton Avenue, Suite 700, Toronto,
Ontario, Canada M4P 2Y3 (a division of Pearson Penguin Canada Inc.)
Penguin Books Ltd, 80 Strand, London WC2R 0RL, England
Penguin Ireland, 25 St Stephen's Green, Dublin 2, Ireland
(a division of Penguin Books Ltd)
Penguin Group (Australia), 250 Camberwell Road, Camberwell,
Victoria 3124, Australia (a division of Pearson Australia Group Pty Ltd)
Penguin Books India Pvt Ltd, 11 Community Centre, Panchsheel Park,
New Delhi - 110 017, India
Penguin Group (NZ), Cnr Airborne and Rosedale Roads, Albany,
Auckland 1310, New Zealand (a division of Pearson New Zealand Ltd)
Penguin Books (South Africa) (Pty) Ltd, 24 Sturdee Avenue, Rosebank,
Johannesburg 2196, South Africa

Penguin Books Ltd, Registered Offices: 80 Strand, London WC2R 0RL, England

10 9 8 7 6 5 4 3 2 1

Copyright 2005 © Gabrielle Charbonnet
All rights reserved

Interior design by Christopher Grassi

Library of Congress Cataloging-in-Publication Data is available

Printed in the United States of America

With love to Fiona Morgan,
who supports me in so many ways.

Clio

I heard a faint sound behind me and froze, my hands inside my canvas bag. I waited, sending my senses out more strongly, but felt nothing out of the ordinary: only sleeping birds, neighborhood dogs and cats, mice. Insects.

Ick.

I let out a deep breath. It was a new moon, which meant this cemetery was even blacker than usual. I was tucked into a remote corner, kneeling on the grass between two tall crypts. I was invisible from all directions, unless someone was right in front of me.

It was almost midnight. I had school tomorrow and knew I would feel like crap in the morning. Too bad. This was my chance, and I wasn't going to waste it.

Quickly and silently I drew a five-foot circle on the ground with sand. Inside the circle, I set four red candles at the four compass points. Red for blood, lineage, passion, fire. I was in the very center, with a small stone bowl filled with chunks of coal in front of me. I lit the candles and the coal, blowing on the coal until it was glowing red.

Then I sat back, gently rested my hands palms up on my knees, and tried to calm my nerves. If Nan woke up and found me gone, I would be dead meat. Or if anyone else found out what I was doing, again, there would be much of the brouhaha.

But two nights ago, at a circle for Récolte, I'd been blown to the ground by a huge surge of power. My own power had been taken and used by someone else. I was still pissed at Daedalus for doing it. So here I was, trying to find out how he'd done it.

I'd practiced magick, the *métier*, pretty much my whole life. I hadn't had my rite of ascension yet, but I'd had great teachers and knew I was pretty powerful for my age. I'd seen any number of grown-ups work magick, for years. But I'd never seen anything like what had happened at Récolte.

Where had Daedalus's power come from? Was it from being immortal? Tonight I was going to try to go to the source: my memory. For some reason, my sister, Thais, and I could tap into memories of our ancestors, the line of witches twelve generations long that led back to the rite, the first rite, the one where the Treize became immortal and Cerise Martin had died.

I'd *seen* what had happened that night. At the time I'd been too freaked to see the big picture. But now that I knew what it was, what had happened, I would find out *how*.

I stilled my whirling thoughts and focused on the burning coal. Fire was my element, and I concentrated on the glowing red heat, feeling it warming the heavy air. On the ground I drew different runes:

2

ôte, for birthright and inheritance, *rad*, for my journey, *lage*, for knowledge and psychic power. I slowed my breathing. The barriers between myself and the rest of the world slowly dissolved; our edges blurred. I took on an awareness of everything around me: the inhalation of a blade of grass, the microscopic release of old, weathered marble on a tomb. In my mind I chanted a spell, one that I'd spent the last two days crafting. It was in English, and I'd totally given up on trying to make it rhyme.

> Chains of time, pull me back
> Let me sink into memory
> Follow the red thread of my blood
> Back through the ages
> Woman after woman, mother after mother
> Giving birth, succumbing to death
> Back to the first one, Cerise Martin
> And the night of Melita's power.
> Show me what I need to know.

I had never done anything like this before, never worked a spell this big. Also, I was deliberately invoking a memory of someone I knew to be evil—Melita Martin, my ancestor. In my earlier visions of that night, I'd been both terrified and horrified at what I'd seen. Now I was going there voluntarily. No one with any sense would think that was okay. But part of being a witch was having an ever-present thirst for knowledge, a desperate need to have questions answered, an overwhelming desire to understand as much as possible.

3

Of course, part of being a witch was also accepting the fact that there were many, many questions that could never be answered and many things that would never be known.

I began singing my song, my unique call for power. I sang it very, very softly—this cemetery was in the middle of an uptown neighborhood, not far from my house, and was bordered by four narrow residential streets. Anyone walking by might hear. A thin shell of awareness was distracting me—I still felt the damp grass I sat on, heard the faint drone of distant grasshoppers.

Maybe this wouldn't work. Maybe I wasn't strong enough. Maybe I had crafted the spell wrong. *Maybe I should ask Melita for help.*

That last thought startled me, and I blinked.

It was sunny, and I was standing in the middle of a small garden patch. I held my long apron up with one hand, and with the other I picked tomatoes, letting them slide into the pouchy sling my apron made. I saw that fat green tomato worms were eating some of the vines. So my anti-tomato-worm spell hadn't worked. *Maybe I should ask Melita for help.*

But now I had enough tomatoes for Maman's gumbo. I hitched up my apron so they wouldn't spill and headed back to the kitchen. My bare feet felt the warm earth, the slightly cooler grass, the rough, packed oyster shells of the path to the barn. My back hurt. My big belly stuck out so I could hardly see my feet. Two more months and the baby would be born. Maman said my back wouldn't hurt anymore then.

4

I'd heard the English looked down hard on a girl unwed but with child. Our village was more accepting. Maman did want me to choose Marcel, to make my own family with him. But I wanted to stay here, in this house, with Maman and my sister. Papa had left long ago, and since then, we were only women here. I liked it that way.

I climbed up the wooden steps to the back room. We cooked outside, everyone did, but we kept our kitchen things in the workroom. Maman and my sister were inside.

"Here." I lifted the tomatoes onto the table, then sat down in a wooden chair, feeling the relief of not carrying the extra weight.

"The *bébé* grows big, no?" my sister said, going to the pail of drinking water on the bench. She dipped me up some, filling a cup, and brought it to me. "Poor Cerise."

"Thanks." The water was warm but good.

Melita knelt in front of me and put her hands on the hard mound of my stomach. She soothed the tight muscles, and her movements calmed the baby, who was active and kicking. One big kick made me gasp, and Melita laughed and tapped the plain outline of a tiny foot.

"You're full of life," she murmured, and smiled up at me, her eyes as black as mine were green, her hair dark like Papa's.

I smiled at her, then caught a glimpse of Maman's face as she snapped green beans. She was worried, watching us. Worried about me and the baby, about Melita and her magick. People said that she worked dark magick, that she risked her soul pursuing evil. I didn't believe them and didn't want to think about it. She was my sister.

"Are you ready for the special circle tonight?" Melita asked, starting to chop tomatoes.

I made a face. "I'm tired—maybe I'll stay home and sleep."

"Oh no, *cher*," she said, looking distressed. "I need you there. It's a special circle, one that will guarantee a time of plenty for the whole village. You must come. You're my good luck charm."

"Who else is going?" I bent down with difficulty and picked up some sewing from the basket. I'd begun making baby dresses, baby hats, baby socks. I carried a girl; I could feel her. Now I was working on a small blanket for the cradle.

"Well, Maman," said Melita.

I glanced at Maman to see her frowning. She, too, was unsure about this circle of Melita's.

"Ouida," Melita cajoled. "You like her. And cousin Sophie. Cousin Luc-Andre. Manon, the smith's daughter."

"That little girl?" Maman asked.

"She wants to take part in more circles," Melita answered. "Um . . ."

The way she hesitated made me look up. "Who else?"

"Marcel," she admitted.

I nodded and went back to sewing. Marcel was a dear. He was so anxious about the baby. Had asked me to marry him a thousand times. I cared about him, truly, and knew he would make a good husband. I just didn't want a husband. He'd been so sure that I'd marry him when I knew I was going to have the baby. But why would I bother marrying when I had Maman and Melita to help me?

"Several others," Melita said, sweeping the chopped tomatoes into a bowl. "It will be perfect. I've been crafting this spell for a long time. I assure you it will bring a long and healthy life to everyone who participates."

"How can you know that?" Maman asked.

Melita laughed. "I've crafted it to be so. Trust me."

At sundown Maman and I walked from our little house to the place Melita had told us about, deep in the woods, not far from the river. I had rested and felt fine and healthy. I couldn't wait for two months to be past so I could meet my baby girl. Would she have light eyes or dark? Fair skin or warm tan? I looked forward to her fatness, her perfect baby skin. Maman had delivered many babies, and I knew it would be hard, but not horrible. And Melita would help.

"Through here," Maman murmured, holding back some trailing honeysuckles. Their strong sweetness perfumed the air, filling my lungs with scent. It was hot and humid and our clothes stuck to us, but everything felt fine.

We reached a small clearing, in front of what Melita had described as the biggest oak tree in Louisiana.

"Holy Mother," Maman breathed, looking at the tree.

I laughed when I saw it—it reached the sky, taller than any tree I'd ever seen. It was so big around that five people holding hands still could not encircle it. It was awe-inspiring, such a monument to how the Mother nourished life. I touched the bark with my palm, almost able to feel the life pulsing under its skin.

"How could I have not known this was here?" Maman said, still gazing at it.

"Petra," said a voice in greeting. "Cerise."

It was remarkable, how I felt chills down my back when I heard his voice or knew that he was near.

Maman turned to him with a smile. "Richard, *cher*. How are you? Melita didn't tell us you were coming."

I turned slowly, in time to see him take off his hat and brush it against one leg. "Melita is very persuasive," he said, not looking at me.

"Petra." Ouida called to her from across the clearing, and, smiling, Maman went to hug her.

I looked into Richard's dark eyes. "Did Melita tell you what this was about?"

"No. You?"

I shook my head and looked for a place to sit. Finally I just sat on the grass, smoothing out my skirts and arching my back to stretch my stomach muscles. "She said it was about ensuring a time of plenty for the village," I said. "Long lives for everyone. I didn't want to come, but she said I was her good luck charm."

Richard sat next to me. His knee accidentally brushed mine, and a ripple of pleasure shot up my spine. My mind filled with other memories of pleasure with Richard, and I wriggled a bit and smiled at him. He got that very still, intent expression that always meant I was about to feel good.

Then he turned away, his jaw set, and I sighed. He was continuing to be upset about Marcel. Just like Marcel was very upset about him. Sometimes the two of them made me tired—why should it matter if I wanted both of them? Why should I have to choose? I wouldn't have cared if they'd also wanted to spark some other girl in the village.

I fanned myself with my straw hat and saw that others were arriving. M. Daedalus, the head of our village, was there, and his friend Jules, who'd lived here for ten years now. M. Daedalus had just gotten back from visiting his brother in New Orleans, I remembered hearing. I wondered if he had brought back any fabric for the Chevets' shop. I'd go look tomorrow.

Melita's best friend, Axelle, arrived, slim like a snake, even in her full skirts and sun hat. I smiled and waved at her, and she waved back.

"Greetings," said a voice, and I turned to see Claire Londine stepping through the honeysuckle. She saw me and came to sit down.

"You're as big as a house," she told me, shaking her head. "How do you feel?"

"Fine, mostly," I said.

"I don't see why you would—" she began, then looked at Richard and stopped.

"I'm going to talk to Daedalus," Richard said abruptly, and left.

Claire laughed. "He sensed woman talk coming on. I wanted to say, why did you let this happen? It's so easy to prevent it. Or to stop it, if it comes to that."

I shrugged. "I decided I'd like to have a baby. I'm going to call her Hélène."

"But babies are so much work," Claire said. "They scream all the time. They never go away."

"Maman and Melita will help me. And I like babies."

"Well, I hope you do," Claire said, stretching her legs out in the sun. Her bare feet and almost six inches of bare leg were visible below her hem, but Claire had always been scandalous. She was nice to me, though, and she'd been in my class at our tiny village school.

"Everyone," my sister called. "It's time. Let's form a circle."

I stood ungracefully, holding my belly with one hand. It was almost sunset, but at that moment the light winked out, like a snuffed candle. I looked up to see huge, plum-colored clouds sweeping in from the south.

"Storm coming in," I murmured to Maman. "Maybe we should do this another time."

Melita heard me. "No," she said. "Tonight is the

only time I can work this spell—everything is perfect: moon, season, people. I'm sure the storm won't bother us."

She quickly drew a large circle that almost filled the clearing, then lit thirteen candles—one for each of us. The wind picked up a bit, an oddly cool, damp wind, but though their flames whipped right and left, the candles stayed lit.

Melita drew the rune *borche* in the air, for new beginnings, birth. I frowned slightly, holding my big stomach. Was that safe? I glanced at Maman. She was watching Melita very solemnly. Maman would stop this or send me away if it wasn't safe. I tried to relax as we all joined hands.

Marcel couldn't take his eyes off me, which irritated me. His gaze was like a weight. Unlike that of Richard, who was across the circle, talking in a low voice with Claire. He laughed, and Claire giggled and swung his hand in hers.

We started to move dalmonde, and Melita began chanting. Again I glanced at Maman and again she had her eyes locked on my sister. I didn't recognize this song—I'd never heard it before, and it didn't match any of our usual forms. Melita's voice became stronger and stronger, seeming to fill my chest. It was very strange—not at all like other circles.

Rain began to fall, big, cool drops soaking my shoulders and the top of my stomach. I vaguely wanted to stop, wanted to let go, but as soon as I thought it, the idea was out of my mind, and Melita's song was filling me again.

My hat flew off as we went faster. I felt awkward, unbalanced, and feared falling, but Jules's and Ouida's hands held me up. Then my throat seemed to close. Huge, heavy, powerful magick welled out of the ground as if it would swallow me up. Of course I'd felt magick before. But this was unlike anything I'd ever even dreamed of. This was overwhelming, an enormous wave made of earth and air and water and fire all at once. I was choking, truly afraid now, and still we circled the hissing candles, Melita's voice filling the air as if it were coming from somewhere else.

Rain poured down. People's faces blurred, smeared images flashing by. Every face except Melita's was afraid—some were angry, also. Thunder rolled through us, so deep that it rocked the earth. The sky was white with lightning, again and again turning us into sharp-edged indigo outlines. I was drowning in magick, caught in magick like a spiderweb, like pitch. I shook my hands to release them but couldn't.

"Meli—" I cried, but at that moment, the world seemed to end. A cannon boom of thunder and an unearthly blast of lightning struck at the same moment. The lightning hit Melita directly and I screamed, seeing her dark hair flying out around her ecstatic face. The next second, the lightning imploded in me, shooting through Jules's hand, searing mine, and racing into Ouida's hand. We all cried out, and I heard my own scream.

An agonizing, gripping pain seized my belly. Our hands flew apart and I fell to the ground. My stomach felt as though someone had buried an ax in it, and I curled up, gasping.

"Maman!" I cried, sobbing. I held my stomach as though to keep my insides from spilling out, but the pain was too big for my hands, too horrendous to bear.

Then others were around me—Richard, Ouida, and finally, Maman, who knelt quickly on the rain-soaked muddy ground. She smoothed my hair off my forehead, her lips already chanting spells. Her hand gripped mine tightly and I clung to it.

"What's happening?" I cried. Maman's strong face filled my eyes, but she muttered spells and didn't answer.

Another searing wave of pain crested, and I closed my eyes and sobbed, trying to ride it out. I felt a gushing flood beneath my skirt, and then Maman's hands were pushing it out of the way and rain hit my bare legs. Richard grabbed my other hand. I pressed it against my cheek, ashamed to be crying and looking weak but too panicked and in pain to stop. Maman and I had already rehearsed the calming and concentrating spells I would perform for the baby's birth, but every one of them fled my mind. All I knew was a dark tide of pain crashing over me, submerging me in its depths.

My stomach was heaving, contracting, and after an eternity, I slowly realized that the pain was less. I felt far away, tired, hardly aware of what was happening.

"Oh goddess, the blood," I dimly heard Ouida say.

13

I knew Richard was still holding my hand, but the pressure was faint. I was so glad that the pain had lessened, so glad that I was removed from the horror and fear and agony. I needed to rest. My eyes closed. Rain splashed my eyelids. The storm still rumbled overhead, but the ground beneath me felt safe and nurturing. I relaxed, feeling all the tension leaving my body. Thank the goddess the pain was gone. I felt perfectly well.

Then I was looking down on myself, on Maman and Richard and the others, looking down from a high distance. I saw the rain drenching everyone. Maman held up a tiny, writhing baby, its blood being washed away by the rain. I saw myself, looking peaceful and calm, as if asleep. *My baby, Hélène*, I thought.

I came out of it when I fell backward and hit my head on a rock.

Blinking, I looked up and saw dark, moonless sky and the tops of family crypts.

My head hurt and I put up a hand to rub it, feeling a knot forming on the back of my skull. I sat up. A chunk of a nameplate had fallen off a crypt, who knew how long ago, and I'd whacked my head against it. I didn't know why I had fallen—if I was dead, why did my head hurt? And my hands?

It took another minute for it to sink in that I wasn't dead; I wasn't Cerise. I was me, Clio, in the here and now. My four candles were guttering and almost out. The small bowl of coal was nothing but gray ashes. I looked around quickly, placing myself, then crawled over to my canvas bag and pulled out my watch. It was 4 a.m. I felt shaken and breathless. This time, instead of just seeing the rite happen, I'd been part of it. I'd heard the spell Melita had used, seen the glowing sigils and runes on the ground, the ones we hadn't seen her write, because she'd put them there before the circle gathered.

I'd felt myself die.

I swallowed, sucking in a shallow, trembling breath, then started to gather my things. I dumped the ashes onto the ground and rubbed them with my toe to make sure they were out. I snuffed the candles and cleaned up the wax that had dripped off.

"Petra would be very displeased if she knew about this."

The dry, slow voice made me jump about a foot in the air. I hadn't sensed anyone around me—still didn't, in fact. Looking around wildly, I finally saw a black shadow sitting on the stoop of a crypt, next to a cement vase holding faded plastic flowers. Daedalus stood and came over to me.

My heart was beating fast—but I put my shoulders back, shook my hair out of my face, and began coolly putting my supplies into my bag.

"You don't care what Petra thinks? She raised you." He knelt a few feet away from me, his black clothes blending into the night.

"Why don't you let me worry about that?" I said. I forced my breathing to slow, kept my face blank.

"Why are you stirring up the past?"

I looked at him. "You saw what I was doing?"

"A bit. Not a lot. It was an ambitious spell. Why were you working it?"

"Why should I tell you?" I stood up, my knees shaky, and shoved my feet into my slides. I began to head for the cemetery gate.

"I could help you."

I paused for just a second, then kept walking. Daedalus walked beside me.

"I could help you," he repeated. "I know more about Melita's spell than anyone. You obviously have a connection to her, through your bloodline. We could combine our strengths. It could be . . . very interesting. Very rewarding."

I reached the rusty wrought-iron gate that led out of the cemetery and opened it. It squeaked loudly.

"I don't think so," I said. "Nan doesn't trust you, and neither do I." I turned and walked away from him, hoping he wouldn't follow me home and maybe wake Petra up to fink on me.

"Think about it." His quiet words floated through the night, but when I turned, he was gone.

Thais

"Chip?" Sylvie held out a bag of Fritos and shook it. It was lunchtime, but our school's cafeteria was always crowded and noisy, so me, my friend Sylvie, her boyfriend, Claude, and Kevin LaTour were sitting outside.

I took some. "Thanks. Trade you for my pickle?"

"Great." Sylvie leaned against Claude and bit the pickle. "At least it's Wednesday," she said. "Middle of the week. After this, it's all downhill, toward the weekend."

I laughed. "I hope next weekend is better than last weekend," I said without thinking.

Next to me, Kevin groaned and covered his face, obviously thinking about our date last Saturday, when we'd gotten hit by lightning. God, and that wasn't even what I'd been talking about. That had been scary, but at least it had been scary in the normal way of just being one of those freaky nature things that happened in New Orleans, not some kind of magickal attack.

"I promise," he said, putting his hand over his heart. "Our next date will be disaster-free."

I slapped his knee lightly. "It wasn't your fault."

Actually, I'd been referring to the nightmare of a Récolte circle I'd gone to on Sunday—but for a second I'd forgotten that I couldn't talk about it with my friends. They knew that witches existed, in a vague way, but they didn't know that I and my family actually practiced the craft.

I still found it hard to believe, myself.

Kevin put his arm around me, and I smiled at him. He was a sweetheart—the more I knew him, the more things I liked about him. Plus, of course, the high adorableness quotient.

"Can you maybe grab some coffee with me after school today?"

My face lit up and then instantly fell. "'Fraid not. First I'm going to get my Louisiana driver's license, then I have to go home and wash, scrape, air out."

Kevin made a sympathetic face. Pretty much every day for the past couple of weeks, my sister Clio and I had spent most waking moments helping to repair, clean, and desmoke our little house. We'd set it on fire during a spell, and the whole back had been damaged.

"But this weekend?" I suggested. "I'm pretty sure if I whine enough, I could possibly get out for one night."

Kevin grinned and kissed my hair. "Just tell me when."

I smiled and nodded, amazed at how normal I was being. Inside, I was still trapped on an emotional Tilt-A-Whirl. It was hard to know which end was up nowadays, with everything that was going on. The best thing about Sylvie, Claude, and Kevin was how unconnected they were to my other life, the life of my new family. With them I could be just Thais Allard, unassuming high school senior, northern transplant. At home I loved being a sister and a sort of grand-daughter, but home was also where magick was made, where my troubling and surreal history seemed unavoidable. At home we talked about what had happened at Récolte, or the autumn solstice. We talked about the fact that some people we knew and were related to were immortal. Literally. And we worried about the rite that Daedalus was planning, the one that might kill me or Clio or make us immortal too.

"I'm sorry, what?" I said, realizing that my friends were looking at me expectantly.

"Did you study for calc?" Sylvie asked again.

I let out a breath. Lovely normalcy. "Yep," I said. "But I still don't get most of it."

"Feel the life in every handful of dirt." My teacher, Melysa, paused to admire the black earth trickling through her fingers.

I looked at her sourly. Gardening was one of my least-favorite things to do, and in our climate you can grow *something* all year round. Plus, the firefighters had completely trampled Nan's gorgeous front beds to get to the back of the house. So here I was, gardening my little heart out, as penance.

And as part of my lesson.

"Yeah, full of life," I muttered, wiping the sweat off my brow. "Gotcha." I leaned over and pulled up a dead plant by the roots. I threw it on the pile to compost and raked the dirt smooth. On the sidewalk sat a tray of eight tiny cabbage plants, waiting to be transplanted. Great. Gardening *and* looking forward to eating cabbage this winter. Oh, joy.

I stood up, stretching and groaning. "I feel like my back is about to break." Not to mention my hands, which were red, as if sunburned, and still stung from last night.

Melysa shot me an amused glance. "Number one, you've only been at it for fifteen minutes. Give me a break. Number two, you're seventeen years old. You don't get to complain about aches and pains until you're fifty. Now, do you remember green cabbage's true name?"

I looked at it. Not napa cabbage or red cabbage, but this particular kind of green cabbage. "*Seste*," I said.

"Very good." Melysa crouched on the ground and dug a small hole with a trowel. Expertly she flipped a cabbage plant out of its plastic cell and popped it in the ground, patting the dirt around it firmly. "Have you been working on a spell for your rite of ascension?"

I blinked at the change in subject. "Uh-huh." *If you only knew,* I thought uncomfortably. She couldn't know, I reassured myself. No one but Daedalus knew about the spell I had done last night in the cemetery.

I raked and pulled, lost in thought. For my rite of ascension, I needed to craft a major spell, one utilizing several levels of power, several forms of spellcrafting, several witch's tools. Last night, I had done just that, and it had worked. It had been the first major magick I had done alone. It had been awful and scary. But I had learned more about what had happened with the Treize. And with Richard, I remembered, feeling my cheeks flush more. As Cerise, I had memories of him as a lover. It felt weird and uncomfortable, as if I had spied on him. Which I guess I had, in a way.

A totally bizarre, unbelievable, *X-Files* kind of way.

But whatever. What was important was that I'd gotten a bird's-eye view of Melita's spell. I'd seen the sigils and runes that had glowed on the ground around the circle. Cerise hadn't been aware of them that night—I wondered if anyone had noticed them, with everything else going on. Cerise dying. But in my vision I had seen them. I had a more complete picture of what Melita had done, and I thought I understood how and why it had worked. But I needed to do more research. Especially with Daedalus still plowing forward with his plans to re-create the rite.

I'd been thinking a lot about immortality. The idea had planted its roots in my mind and was taking firmer hold. What would things be like two hundred years from now? What would it be like to never fear death? I didn't know exactly how it worked—like, could one of the Treize jump off a cliff and just get up afterward, like Wile E. Coyote? What would it be like to be frozen in time as I was now—young and strong and beautiful? I would never age, never get gray hair and wrinkles and have things droop on me. I would be able to learn magick my whole life. What would my powers be like a hundred years from now, with a hundred years of studying under my belt? Would I just keep getting stronger?

It was starting to sound pretty damn good.

But—would Thais agree with me? Could I bear to become immortal while she went on to age and die? True, I'd had a sister for only a few months, but she was my mirror image. It would be like watching myself age and die. Now that we knew each other, we were joined. We were connected. It deepened with every day that passed. Could I bear for that connection to be broken someday?

Next to me, Melysa planted the other baby cabbages. I finished preparing my bed and knelt down to sprinkle weensy radish seeds in short rows. It was almost October, but we had plenty of time for another radish crop. And cabbages grew well in chillier temperatures. Like, if it got down in the fifties. I sighed and brushed my hair off my neck.

"Feel free to share," Melysa said.

I looked up. "Oh. Well—I've just been thinking about different things," I said. "Listen—do you understand the form of the Treize's original spell?"

Melysa looked surprised. She was the only non-Treize member who knew about Nan and her *famille*, knew their freakish history.

"Well, a bit," she said. "I don't know if anyone truly understands all its nuances or powers. Not even the people . . . who were there."

Daedalus says he does, I thought. *He says he knows enough to re-create it.*

And he wants to teach me.

I pushed that thought out of my mind.

"But what would the basic form be?" I persisted.

Melysa frowned slightly as she cut several small squashes off the vine growing on our fence. "Why do you want to know?"

"I'm just curious. It seems so amazing, so out of the realm of what we usually do."

Her eyes were serious when they met mine.

"It is," she said. "For good reason. That kind of magick isn't positive, doesn't add a positive presence to the world. It's harmful, it creates an unnatural situation, it affects other people without their will or knowledge. It's forbidden."

"Forbidden? Do people even know enough about it to outlaw it? Wasn't that spell with the Treize the only instance of it?"

Melysa, who I could usually ask almost anything, took on an uncharacteristically shuttered expression. She didn't answer, and a flash of excitement rushed through me. Did that mean there had ever been other spells like Melita's? Was there a whole school of magick that I—and most witches—knew nothing about? It would be incredibly interest—

Oh. Yes. Now I got it. Yes, there was a whole school of magick that probably dealt with spells similar to Melita's. It was called dark magick, and we did not practice it. It had never occurred to me that among all the awful, evil, totally wrong spells of dark magick, there would be some that could work a spell like Melita's. The kind of spell that would grant immortality to the witches present.

And that could kill a witch too, I remembered, trying not to shudder at the memory of feeling Cerise die.

I heard the familiar cheerful chugging of my little Camry and looked up. Thais had found a parking space in the street right in front of our house—we didn't have a driveway or garage. She got out and walked through our gate, careful not to step on any plants.

"So, you got it?" I asked.

She smiled, looking exactly like me except for the clothes, and waved her new Louisiana driver's license.

"I'm legal now. To drive, anyway." She surveyed the front yard, which was being transformed from a trampled, sooty, demilitarized zone into a mere inkling of the glory of Nan's old garden. "You guys have gotten a lot done. Let me change and I'll come help for a while before dinner."

"Great, thanks," said Melysa, smiling at her.

Having an identical twin sister was starting to feel a teensy bit more normal, but waves of "this is unbelievable" still flitted through my head. I'd spent seventeen years as an only child—having my entire world turned inside out in the last couple of months had made me feel like I was tripping sometimes.

"What's that?" Thais asked, pointing to the baby cabbages. "Not more okra?"

I laughed. Thais was still getting her south-erner's taste buds jump-started.

"Cabbage!" I said brightly, and she made a face.

Melysa stood and brushed off her hands. "It's time I was going, now that you've got a helper. Tell Petra I'll talk to her later, all right?"

"Okay. Thanks—see you soon." I stood up and followed Thais inside. It was time I found out exactly what she thought about immortality.

Black Like My Soul

This had all changed so much. Except for the heat, the mosquitoes, the smell of the water. Those were the same. But the way the land looked, the contours of the canals and the rice fields and the rivers themselves—all that was different. The small trolling motor on this old wooden pirogue made an annoying buzzing sound, like a big, sleepy insect. Richard sat in the stern, one hand on the tiller, maneuvering his way through water paths that had changed ten times since he'd seen them. How long ago had he been here, to this very place? Maybe forty years? Thirty? Decades blended together.

The sun was hot on his skin, warming his blood. Richard brushed his damp bangs off his forehead and lit a cigarette. He remembered Clio snootily telling him not to smoke in Petra's house. He guessed Petra hadn't told Clio she herself had smoked for roughly eighty years. He snorted smoke out his nose, feeling the heat, the chemical aftertaste.

Up there. A quarter mile ahead, the flat, treeless rice fields gave way to a flat swamp. The canal was about to become choked with weeds, so Richard shut off the motor and pulled it in. He got out a long, broad paddle, its paint worn away, and began pushing through the weeds. Water hyacinths. Really pretty, shiny green leaves, pretty purple flowers. Clogging canals, ditches, and rivers throughout the Gulf states.

But pretty.

Like Clio.

She too was pretty and useless—in fact, destructive. Look what she had done to Petra's house. At least, he was pretty sure it had been her, her and Thais's spell going wrong. *Unless* . . . Frowning, Richard flicked his cigarette into the water. There was a quick hiss, and then Richard remembered that littering was verboten nowadays. Damn.

He took off his shirt and began to push the pirogue through the thick weeds. He saw a nutria, as big as a house cat, race across the canal where the hyacinths were so thick they could practically support its weight.

Twenty minutes later he was clear of the canal and started the motor again. There was an almost-hidden entrance along here, leading to a narrow, snaking river barely twelve feet wide. Here it was. He angled the boat in and cut the motor again. Too many cypress trees and trailing underwater weeds. Easy to chew up your propeller. Most of the trees were new growth, but something about the general contours triggered his memory. This was the place.

Mosquitoes buzzed around him, but he'd done a little spell that kept them off. He took out another cigarette and was about to light it when he remembered Clio's face, her wrinkled nose. Swearing with disgust, he tossed the pack onto the flat bottom of the boat. God, what was the matter with him? She was stuck-up, snide, selfish—and still hung up on Luc, which only showed how stupid she was.

And yet.

When Richard was around her, his heart started beating again, and he suddenly felt more alive than he had in a hundred years. He remembered her long, bare, tan legs, stretched across the kitchen floor as she cleaned inside a cabinet. He remembered her in russet linen, the fabric floating across her stomach, her hips, at the Récolte circle. Something about her made him want to crush her to him, to bend her head over his arm. . . . But it would never happen again. She was out of his system now—those searing kisses at Récolte had cured him of her. He would never touch her again.

Looking up quickly, Richard took his bearings. Had he passed it? He'd been so distracted, thinking about Clio. Swearing again under his breath, he peered ahead, trying to see around the next bend. No. This wasn't it. He'd gotten lost.

It took a seven-point turn to get the pirogue facing the other direction. Richard glanced at the sun—he had a couple more hours before the boat's owner would return and notice it was missing. Richard began to paddle, putting his back into it. He was sweating, the air so still and damp that it couldn't evaporate. He remembered he had a bottle of water and took a long drink, wishing it were beer.

Now he was at the last fork. Looking at it again, he saw he needed to take the other arm. Grimly he put his oar in the water. That was what thinking about Clio would get him. Turned around. Lost. She wanted Luc? She could have him.

Another fifteen minutes of paddling brought him to another juncture. He knew where he was now and unerringly took the left fork. Five minutes later he saw it: a thick, bent, twisted cypress hanging arched over the water like a bow. Long ago a length of chain had been wrapped around its trunk; now it was almost buried beneath the bark. Ducking low, Richard slid the pirogue under the arch. He stepped out into the shallow water, feeling the smooth clay squishing beneath his sandals, and tied the boat to a tree.

The bank was steep but not high, and he pulled himself up it by grabbing tree roots.

He reached the top and headed inland, pushing aside vines and thick underbrush. Again he checked the position of the sun, squinting up through the thick treetops. He had enough time, barely, if he didn't get lost again.

Clio was destroying his peace of mind. Why? She was nothing to him. Another tragedy in a long line of tragedies. Richard had thought he could solve that situation, but now he knew he was powerless. Something occurred to him, and he stood still for a moment, struck. If Clio didn't get over Luc and Luc, that bastard, took advantage of that fact, then Clio could very well end up in the same situation as the twelve generations of women before her. Including Cerise. She could get pregnant. And then she would die.

Two months ago, he hadn't known Clio or Thais. He'd distanced himself from that whole line of doomed women, knowing that he would eventually hear that the latest version of the marked line had died. He would have felt bad for a moment and then shrugged it off.

But now he knew Clio and Thais. Clio was the only woman of that line that he'd wanted, besides Cerise.

A sudden image of Clio's beautiful face flashed through his mind. He saw her green eyes wide with fear, her black hair streaked with sweat, her hands covered with blood. In a split second he pictured her face still and lifeless, her eyes open, all of her wet, soaked through, as if rained on. Dead.

The ground spun beneath him and he dropped to his knees. He closed his eyes, swallowing hard, and leaned forward, resting one hand on the warm ground. Clio dead. He blinked several times, trying to erase the image from his mind. It had been unusually clear and real, like a premonition. Slowly he sat back on his knees, wishing fervently that he hadn't left his smokes back in the frigging boat. He swallowed again and wiped the cold sweat from his forehead. He felt shaky, chilled.

He looked around and cast his senses, making sure he was alone. He felt nothing out of place—just plants and animals and insects. And a very thin, very tremulous thread of ancient magick, vibrating slightly in the air.

He got to his feet and began walking toward it.

He hadn't had a vision like this in ages. It had happened to him only a couple of times in his whole life. The first time had been the afternoon before Melita's circle. He'd been hoeing his father's field, and then suddenly he'd seen Cerise dead. She'd been drenched with rain, and Melita had stood next to her, laughing. Blood was everywhere. In that moment, he'd seen that Cerise would die at the circle that night.

Yet he had gone.

Now he saw one of his landmarks, a granite boulder almost as tall as he. It would never have occured naturally in Louisiana. He looked around and found the second boulder, then the third, forming a rough triangle. The rocks looked as if they'd been here for millennia, and Richard wondered how many casual hikers had seen them and not realized that they were completely out of place.

Inside the triangle, Richard started with the northernmost rock and counted off paces. He aligned his arms with the other two rocks, made a half turn, and counted six more paces. Then he dropped to his knees again, pulled out his folding shovel, and started to dig. With his first hard thrust, the shovel bounced off the dirt and flew up, almost hitting him in the face.

He blinked, surprised for a moment, and then

he smiled ruefully. Under his breath he said a disarming spell. This time the metal blade sank easily into the dark, rich soil. He dumped the shovelful of dirt to one side and pushed his shovel in again, digging further, further into the past.

All the More Believable

He certainly was spending a lot of time in cemeteries these days, Daedalus thought as he walked between two rows of graves. Some of them were simply aboveground cement troughs, built to hold coffins, then backfilled with dirt up to the level of the sides. Not as durable as covered crypts, which were little houses for the dead, but of course cheaper and easier to maintain.

Cemeteries were always so peaceful. And hot. The sunlight bounced off the white marble and soaked into the cement, radiating out for hours after twilight. He didn't feel anyone else's presence here, at least no one he knew, but all the same he detoured past the weathered facade of the Martins' crypt. Petra's husband, Armand. Armand's brother and his wife.

Daedalus had been surprised when Armand had left Petra. Not that they were the picture of wedded bliss, but then who was? Losing all those children had taken a toll on them both, but that had been so common back then, even among witches. It would have been worse without all the protection spells and healing powers. Daedalus had visited New Orleans during those years, and there he'd heard of families losing ten children out of fourteen or every one of their infants, one a year until they gave up in despair.

In his *famille*, they'd known how to prevent or delay the birth of children, and their child mortality rate had been one-tenth that of their region. Still, losing any child felt like too much, Daedalus knew.

He retraced his steps, walking across the cemetery to the side closest to the river. Here was a small wrought-iron bench, somewhat rusted, but still sturdy. He sat on it, his hands moving in an automatic gesture to flip his coattails out of the way. He shook his head at his own foolishness. He was wearing a plain white shirt and gray-and-white seersucker pants. A jacket hadn't been required wear for decades. Old habits died hard.

He sat back, resting his cane against the side of the bench. There had been a time when most people carried canes as a fashion accessory, but Daedalus had gotten his first one when he was barely eighteen. His mule had kicked him hard in the thigh, shattering the bone. Petra had wrought her spells, saving his leg—on anyone else, it would have turned gangrenous and been amputated. But he'd limped. In the 1970s, he'd finally gotten it surgically repaired, but it had taken another fifteen years to learn how to not limp. Now he walked perfectly but still carried a cane. Some habits were too hard to break.

The sun was low enough so that Daedalus sat in

shade. It had been very, very interesting to find Clio Martin working spells last night. Spells he was certain Petra wouldn't have allowed. Spells that sought the origin—or at least an understanding—of Melita's power.

How long it would take before her thirst for power, for knowledge, exceeded her loyalties to Petra? Perhaps not that long.

Closing his eyes, Daedalus muttered a spell. It was the same spell he cast in this place every time he came here. Every few days whenever he was in New Orleans. He opened his eyes, feeling foolish again for his faint air of expectancy.

There was nothing.

Carefully Daedalus looked at the tomb directly in front of him, the tomb of the *famille* Planchon. His family. His parents and most of his other ancestors were buried down in Lafourche Parish, near where their *ville* had been. But not everyone. Daedalus's brother, Jean-Marie, had been buried here twenty years after Daedalus became immortal. Immortal and yet unable to save his favorite brother. Now he came when he could to his brother's grave.

Not once in 250 years had he seen what he'd been looking for: some sign that his brother's wife had come to pay her respects. That didn't mean she hadn't been here, of course. Just that she'd left no sign. And why should she have? She'd never wanted to see any of them again. That night she had left Jean-Marie as surely as she had left all of them, and

Jean-Marie had never heard from her again. Or at least, not that he had ever admitted to Daedalus.

Then he had died.

The bottom of the inch-thick marble faceplate had broken off and lay in big pieces on the ground. He really should have it repaired or replaced. He read the words, as he had read them thousands of times before, and they made no more sense now than they did when he'd first paid to have them engraved.

Jean-Marie Planchon. Born: 1731. Died: 1783. Beloved brother of Daedalus Planchon. Faithful husband to Melita Martin.

Taught by Evil

Time had stretched out into an unending emotional and physical pain that might very well drive him mad, Marcel thought. It had been almost three days since he'd been summoned. It had taken this long to get his passport in order, acquire a plane ticket, and get to Shannon, the closest airport. Three days of torment, as if spiders were crawling under his skin. The magickal urging of the summoning spell. He would feel increasingly worse until he saw Daedalus.

Now his flight was leaving in half an hour—they were starting to board out on the tarmac. This small plane would take him to London, where he would connect with a flight to New York and then another one to New Orleans.

He threw away his paper cup of tea and picked up his one small leather valise. He felt more out of place than he usually did, surrounded by bright lights, radio noise, children and women as brightly colored as parrots. He longed again for the monastery, with its silence and hushed sounds, the soothing gray stone and worn wood, the deep voices, the ever-present brown robes.

He was reaching for the glass door that led outside when a querulous voice hailed him.

"Father. Bless me, will you, Father?"

Marcel turned to see an old woman, bent with age but still dignified, her silver hair neatly coiled on the back of her head. She approached him with firm steps, sensible brogues seeming like boats on her narrow feet. Her tweed skirt was worn but once of good quality.

She smiled and knelt with difficulty. A gnarled hand reached for the hem of his robe. Before he could stop her, she had kissed it. "Bless me, Father," she murmured, her head bowed.

Marcel felt another pang of sorrow and loss so acute that tears started to his eyes. He had never felt worthy of this traditional demonstration of faith, but now somehow, tainted anew by his past, he felt even more fraudulent.

Kneeling himself, wincing from the exquisite pain of this reminder of everything he was giving up and leaving behind, he took the woman's hand and helped her rise.

"No," he murmured. "I am so unworthy, it's you who should be blessing me. I should kneel at your feet. I am nothing."

The woman's face was uncomprehending as he went on as though talking to himself. "I am worse than nothing, because I am made of evil."

The woman drew back, her faded blue eyes searching his.

He saw her fear and forced himself to smile gently at her. Then he turned and pushed through the glass doors out into the misty rain. *I am made of evil,* he thought sadly, crossing the tarmac to the waiting commuter plane. *I was born in evil, grew into evil, and was taught by evil.*

He climbed the slick metal steps that had been rolled over to the side of the plane. Ducking into the damp-smelling cabin, he saw there were only two passengers besides himself.

He settled into a seat, gazing out his tiny window. He wanted to rush outside and fling himself to the ground, physically holding on to the land of his adopted home.

A flight attendant offered him a drink.

"No, thank you."

Evil. His darkness spoiled everything he touched. He put his head back and closed his eyes, feeling more wretched than he thought possible. Almost as wretched as that night so long ago, when he'd watched Cerise die. Everyone had felt the lightning shoot through them, filling them with light and power, but that same power had killed Cerise as she birthed her daughter. He remembered Melita's triumphant face, flushed and beautiful. She had run off that night. She'd destroyed the huge oak tree and the Source. Marcel had tracked her through the darkness, like a panther. He'd caught up to her, and he'd struck her down. He'd stood there, panting, howling inside with anguish and grief, as Melita lay facedown in the mud. The rain had pelted her dress like bird shot. His heart, his life and love had been destroyed, so it was only fitting that he destroy the cause.

Then Melita had raised her head, had turned to look at him. She'd wiped mud out of her eyes as he'd stared at her, speechless. She had laughed at him.

Enraged, he'd raised his mattock again—but she'd thrown out one arm, speaking dark words that whipped around him like strangle vine. And just like that, she'd taken hold of his soul.

And she'd kept it, for years and years.

Thais

I pulled off my cute school top and searched for an old T-shirt, suitable for drudgery. "How about strawberries?" I asked as Clio came and lounged on my bed. "Planting strawberries—I could get behind that."

"Too late in the season," Clio said.

I rummaged through a drawer. "When will Petra be home?"

Clio groaned. "Who knows? Once she was gone for almost thirty hours, and then one time she went out to a case and was home in an hour. She said the baby just popped out."

I made a face at the mental image, and Clio grinned wryly.

"Listen," she said. "We still have to figure out who was trying to harm us. I mean, it seems like the attacks have maybe stopped, but it would strengthen our position to know who was actually behind them. Let's do another reveal spell before Nan gets home."

"Oh, *that's* a good idea. What else needs burning down?" Last time we had tried working magick, we'd almost destroyed our home.

"Very funny," Clio said, then sat up. "Hey, maybe we should do it right outside Luc's apartment. I bet lightning would hit it or a meteor would drop on it or something."

I tried to smile. Luc was still a very sore subject, despite how hard I was working to put him out of my mind.

"What do you mean, strengthen our position?" I asked. "Our position on what?"

Not answering, Clio raised one arm and trailed it along an Indian-print bedspread that I had hung over my window. It was weird, seeing myself performing these natural but dramatic gestures—like a hyper-feminized me.

I pulled on an ancient tie-dyed T-shirt. "Waiting, here."

Clio looked at me. "The whole immortality thing."

"What about it?" I asked warily.

"Have you been thinking about it? I mean, this whole huge possibility was just dropped into our laps, and we haven't really talked about it."

I stared at her. "Yes, we have. We talked about how we didn't want any part of it, how Daedalus was awful or crazy, how we wanted the Treize to leave us alone."

"No, we didn't," Clio said seriously. "Maybe *you* said something like that, but we haven't really talked it all out. I've been thinking about it more and more."

"Again I ask, what about it?" I wasn't liking the

direction this conversation was taking, and I headed out of my room and went downstairs.

In the kitchen I took an apple from the bowl on the table and bit into it. "Man, apples suck here," I muttered. Clio came in and poured us a couple of glasses of iced tea. She and Petra didn't drink sodas much—they called them soft drinks and never bought them at the store. Maybe they weren't natural enough or something. "You haven't tasted a real apple till you taste an apple in the north, where they're grown."

"Okay, someday I'll make a point of it. Thais, don't you want to be immortal?"

There. She'd said it. Now I couldn't ignore the white elephant in the room. "Well, no."

The expression on her face said she couldn't believe I had said that.

"Thais! Immortality! The more I think about it, the more I want it. I want to freeze right here. I don't ever want to die. And I don't ever want *you* to die."

"I don't want us to die either," I said. "But the idea of the rite terrifies me, especially considering what happened at Récolte! There's no way I would go through the actual rite. We have no idea what could happen!" Wishing she would just drop it, I got up to put more curtains in the washer. Then I paused, suddenly seeing Petra's face in my mind but unsure why.

"I feel—" I began as I heard the front door open. I realized what it had been. "Petra? I sensed you!" I said, amazed. "I sensed you before you came in!"

"Hi, girls," Petra called, heading back to the kitchen.

Excited, I glanced at Clio, but she looked upset and even angry. "We'll talk about this more later," she said, and started loading the dishwasher.

"Pretty cool, huh?" said Petra, entering the kitchen. "You sensed my aura. It's easier the better you know someone, but you can do it with strangers too or even animals if you concentrate."

"Huh," I said, impressed.

"And hello to you too," said Petra, kissing Clio on her cheek. "Your powers are awakening, my dear. As time goes on and you learn more, your powers will increase. Then having a heightened awareness of everything about you will be second nature."

She dropped her large macramé purse in a chair. "I noticed the front garden. You two have been working hard."

"It was Clio," I said. "Clio and Melysa. She said to tell you she'd talk to you later."

Petra poured herself a glass of iced tea and leaned against the counter, looking tired.

"Hard day?" I asked, gathering an armful of curtains off the table. I opened the back door to get to the tiny room attached to the side of the house where we kept our washer and dryer. The outside walls of the little add-on room had been scorched, but luckily the appliances inside were fine.

Back in the kitchen, Petra put her empty glass down. "Yes, it's been a long one," she replied. "I'm going to change. Then we can think about dinner."

Giving us a smile, she went into her small alcove room under the stairs.

"Thais," Clio whispered. "Please, just think about it. This is really important to me. Say you'll think about it."

I sighed. "Okay. I'll think about it."

Clio nodded, then went back out to the front yard.

Leaving me feeling totally uneasy.

Not to Be Trusted

Axelle rang the doorbell. On the second floor, a casement window cranked open, and Sophie leaned out.

"Oh—hi," she said. Axelle knew why she was surprised—she and Sophie and Manon didn't usually socialize. But then again, this wasn't exactly a social call.

"Can I come up?"

In answer, Sophie pressed the buzzer that unlocked the downstairs door.

Upstairs, Axelle looked around. "This is nice," she said. There was one large room, a small kitchen off it, and then a hall that Axelle assumed led to bedrooms. "Do you get tired of moving?" she asked, surprising herself. She didn't usually give a rat's ass about what Sophie or Manon thought.

Manon came down the hall, wearing a short silk dress. Axelle had the fleeting thought of the huge sum Manon could make as a child prostitute, then felt a little abashed. Manon never would, of course. But she *could* make a fortune, and it wasn't like she was actually a child, anyway.

"What's up?" Manon asked, sitting in an arm-chair.

"Axelle just asked if we were tired of moving," Sophie said, seeming confused.

"That's not what I'm here for," Axelle said, sitting on the couch. She leaned back against the arm and put her feet up.

"Do you want something to drink?" Sophie asked politely.

"God, yes," said Axelle. "What do you have?"

"Um, tea or . . . or we have some wine open, and I think we have some Cointreau. Manon was cooking with it."

"A little Cointreau would be nice," said Axelle. "Thanks."

"What's this about our moving?" Manon asked.

"No—I'm here to talk about Daedalus," Axelle said, taking the small glass from Sophie. "Thanks. It's just, when I walked in, I thought about how many apartments I'd lived in over the years, and I had a one-second thought about whether anyone else got tired of moving." Now she felt exhausted, having this stupid conversation. This was why she didn't socialize with Sophie and Manon.

"I get tired of it," said Manon, leaning her head back. Her fair blond hair spread across the chair like in a shampoo commercial. She would have been a knockout as a grown woman. It was too bad.

"There was a place in Provence, before it became popular," Manon went on. "We loved it there." She looked at Sophie, and Sophie smiled and nodded.

"We would have stayed forever, but after a couple of years, people always start to wonder why I'm not getting older."

A dark bitterness lay beneath her words. For the first time it occurred to Axelle that Sophie and Manon might have different agendas. She glanced again at Sophie, saw her face was drawn and sad, though she was trying to hide it. Axelle took a slow sip of her drink, inhaling the intense orange scent, letting the liquid burn slowly down her throat. Frankly, she preferred vodka. Vodka you could just knock back.

"I know what you mean," Axelle said. "The longest I ever stayed in one place was eight years. It gets tiresome, moving all the time." She paused, shifting. Did it matter to her plan if they wanted different things? Should she approach this differently? She didn't know. She was tired of thinking about it. Might as well throw it out there. "So, when Daedalus told me of his plan, of finding the twins—well, it all seemed to make sense to me. We all have something to gain from doing the rite, no? But lately I've been wondering if Daedalus perhaps has some other plan that no one, not Jules nor I, knows about. To tell you the truth, I've been wondering if he can be trusted."

Sophie and Manon just looked at her solemnly.

"And not only him—Petra also. She's so concerned about the twins and their safety that she might not be seeing the big picture. She might not care what Daedalus is up to as long as the girls are safe. I've been worried. I feel like I need a backup plan. Like we all need a backup plan. What do you say?"

"What do we say to what?" Manon asked, eyebrows drawn together.

"Forming an alliance," Axelle said, impatient. "The three of us. If we know that we're guarding each other's backs, we might be able to relax a bit, not worry so much. I mean, we're dealing with the Treize here. Who among them can you trust?"

"Yes, I see," Sophie said slowly.

"I don't know what Daedalus is planning," said Axelle, putting her empty glass on the coffee table. Her stomach felt pleasantly warmed by the Cointreau. "I don't know what anyone is planning. I want to talk to everyone, away from Daedalus. I want us, at least some of us, to be standing together when his plan goes down."

"That makes sense," said Manon, looking at Sophie.

"Well, you think about it," said Axelle, standing up. She smoothed her Lycra skirt over her hips and slipped her feet back into her high-heeled sandals. She remembered the horrible, ugly shoes everyone wore during World War II and shuddered.

"Think about it, talk it over, and let me know, okay?"

"Okay," said Sophie, walking her to the door. "Thanks for coming to talk to us about it."

Axelle paused, one step down, and looked up at Sophie. "You and I are different and always will be," she said. "After this drama is over, we might not speak again for sixty years. For the most part, I don't care what your life is like or what you two do with it. But if this situation is dangerous, if Daedalus is planning to use us for something, the way Melita did, then we need to stand together, tightly together, you know?"

"Yes." Sophie nodded, seeming sad again.

"Okay. So, later." Axelle went down the stairs and out onto the quiet neighborhood street. She took a deep breath, then stopped to light a cigarette. Goddess, that had been hard. It was so much harder to be sincere than to spin a web of half-truths that wouldn't hold up to the light. It was so unnatural. She shook her head, blew out a long stream of smoke, and headed to her car.

Thais would take some convincing. That much was clear. I needed to come up with Thais-like reasons for her to do it. Like, if she were alive long enough, she could figure out how to cure cancer. Something like that. Or if we were immortal, we'd never have to worry about anyone attacking us again. We could laugh at muggers and light posts. How could she not want that, and right *now*?

I would talk to her about it later and maybe do some more research. But first I had my other quest, my other spell.

In my vision of Cerise dying at the rite, I'd seen runes and sigils glowing on the ground for a split second, right before the lightning hit. They had burned like fire. Some of them I'd recognized— some I hadn't. But they all had to do with Melita's spell—

"Clio?"

So much for my sensing skills. I jumped at Nan's voice, then turned to see her in the doorway of my room.

"Sorry—didn't mean to startle you." She looked a bit bemused that she'd been able to.

"Working on my ROA," I said, gesturing to my Book of Shadows, the notes spread everywhere.

"Then I hate disturbing you," she said. "But could you do me a favor? I'm showing Thais some basic centering spells, and I've realized we're all out of blue candles. I really think they'd help."

"You want me to run to Botanika?" I said, loving the idea of getting out.

"Would you? If you get the candles, we can keep working till you get back."

"Yeah, okay," I said, sliding my feet into some kitten-heeled mules. I did it slowly, hoping Nan wouldn't wait for me. She smiled and headed back downstairs, and I whipped over to my bed, shoved all my notes back into my BOS, then spelled it and put it on my desk, very casual looking. I took a page of unknown symbols and stuck it into my miniskirt pocket, then hurried downstairs.

"Back in a few," I said, passing through the workroom.

"Thanks, sweetie," said Nan. "Be extra careful."

"Gotcha." I grabbed my purse and car keys and headed out the front door into the night. It was warm but not awful, and I was thrilled to get out for a while. I'd been so housebound lately, what with all the Cinderella-ing, coupled with the humiliating lack of boyfriend. I mean, I always had *someone* around. But not since I'd met Luc. No, since that whole train wreck, I'd been alone, pathetically advising my sister on date-wear while *I* sat home *knitting*. Okay, well, metaphorically knitting.

I drove down Magazine Street to Botanika. Inside, I got myself an iced latte, then took it into the store section. They had the best collection of occult books in New Orleans, which was saying something.

First I looked in the spellcraft section. I found a couple of books that were a bit over my head, but even they dealt with spell forms I'd heard of before: the basic "cast circle, call on elements, delineate spell and its limitations, call power, enact spell, disband." Familiar stuff and then some variations, including an interesting one that relied on natural limitations, like phases of the moon. It seemed somewhat risky to me, but nothing hit me as very dangerous or dark or super-powerful.

I glanced around, but no one was paying attention to me. There was another, restricted area of the book section: a short, dark passageway lined with bookshelves. At one end was a fire exit. A gold cord and a sign blocked entrance from the store. *Not open to minors, due to the sensitive nature of the works within.*

I slipped under the cord. My eyes adjusted almost immediately to the dim light.

Small, faded paper labels identified some shelves. There were sections for Biography, Spellcraft, Grimoires, Books of Shadows, Witch's Tools, Tantric Power, and so on. *Biography of a Dark Witch* was one title, and my eyes widened with interest. But first I needed to see what else was here. *Don't Invoke Danger* seemed pretty forbidding. There were more: *Celestial Omens, Personal Power, The Thin Line Between Light and Dark*, and one titled simply *Dark Magick*.

All of them looked incredible, and I couldn't believe I'd never been in here before. Actually, I wasn't sure they would sell me any of them anyway. I could try. But I wasn't finding anything about immortality, channeling lightning, or something. I would know it when I saw it.

I didn't have much time. Nan would give me only so long, then call my cell phone, worried. I would have to come back another time. Quickly I stooped down and looked at the dark-spined books on the lower shelves. Many of them were in different languages. Curious, I pulled out one called *Mastering Life*, which I thought might be about immortality. It kind of was, but it didn't seem to parallel Melita's spell in any way.

A book called *Forbidden Symbols* caught my eye, and I pulled it out. Flipping through it, I saw one and then two of the unknown sigils from my vision. I tucked the book under my arm. I would try to buy it, and if they wouldn't sell it to me, then I'd come back later and copy its information. I was about to leave when I saw a thin, falling-apart volume shoved toward the back of one shelf. I could see it only from above—at eye level the other book's spine covered it. I eased it out carefully, its binding practically crumbling in my hands. Once it had been dark red, but now it was so old and grimy, it was almost black. I opened the cover.

Being the Personal History of One Hermann Parfitte; and How He Learned to Subvert the Power of Others, I read silently. Subvert the power of others? Bingo. That was more like what Melita had done. I tucked that book under my arm too and stood, and just as I did, a rush of heat and awareness made me think— Richard.

I whirled and saw . . . Luc. Watching me from the entrance of the restricted area. As usual, a flush rose in my cheeks and my heart started beating fast. Keeping my face neutral, I walked right toward him and ducked under the cord, forcing him to step aside. I brushed past him and headed for the candle section.

He followed me.

"What do you have there, Clio?" he said. His voice was beautiful, slightly accented, and reminded me of afternoons we'd spent lying in each other's arms.

"Candles." I chose some off the shelf, making sure they were unscented and the right diameter.

"The books," he said, and reached for them, his fingers brushing my side.

A tingling shock went through me, as if I had touched a live wire. I tried to pull away, but the books slipped out from under my arm. Luc read the titles, his eyelashes thick and dark as he looked down.

"None of your business," I said coolly. "Just like every other aspect of my life."

He looked up at me, his handsome face thoughtful. "How are you?" he asked, not commenting on the books. "Have you recovered from Récolte?" He'd been furious at the Récolte circle—he'd punched Daedalus, knocking him to the ground.

I took my books back, practically snatching them out of his hands. Inside, I felt trembly, uncertain, hurt. All the usual Luc feelings. I wondered if he wished he'd run into Thais instead.

Not answering him, I headed to the checkout counter. I hated this. I loved him, but he loved my sister. He was still everything I wanted. Why was he playing games with me? What could he possibly get out of it now?

The clerk rang up my candles and started to ring up the books. She paused when she saw the red RESTRICTED stamp on the inside, by the handwritten price. Looking up at me, she seemed to weigh her options. She'd been working here for several months, and I knew she was Wiccan. Not everyone who worked here was a witch, but she was. She said, "Are you over eighteen?" She looked barely over eighteen herself, with her turquoise hair, pierced nose, and tattooed arm.

"Yes," I said clearly, wanting to will her into believing it but figuring it probably wouldn't work.

"Can I see some ID?"

Crap. Damn it. How freaking embarrassing, right in front of Luc. I really needed these books, had to have them. I didn't want to come back—

"Those are mine." Luc stepped up to the counter and put down some money and a driver's license.

The clerk glanced from Luc to me while I held

my breath. Luc looked only a little older than I did—he'd been frozen in time when he was nineteen. He would be carded in bars forever.

The clerk finished ringing up my candles and handed me my change. She looked at Luc's license, rang up the books separately, and put them in a plain paper bag. Handing it to Luc, she gave us both steady looks, as if to say, "I hope you know what you're doing."

Outside, in the night air, I took the books back from Luc. "Thanks," I said ungraciously, and held out a twenty.

He shook his head, waving it away. "Those books are dangerous, little Clio. Why do you want them?"

I turned to head for my car, but his warm hand on my shoulder, heating my skin right through my shirt, made me stop. I loved the way his hands felt on me. A wave of longing and attraction washed over me, practically making me whimper.

Slowly he turned me to face him. "What are those books for? Or . . . who?"

I shrugged. Who else would they be for? He didn't think Petra would want these titles, did he?

"Tell me. I might be able to help you."

The thought of making magick with him made me want to cry. This was unbearable. I pulled my shoulder away. "You've already done enough," I said, my voice shaky, and headed back to my car.

But again, as I was reaching for the door, Luc turned me to face him. I stood as he traced my cheek with his fingers, burning trails of awareness wherever they touched. He put his head close to mine, and I thought I would scream.

"I miss you," he said softly, gently raising my chin to look into my eyes. He pushed his other hand through my hair, holding the back of my neck. "I'm so sorry I hurt you." Then he lowered his lips to my temple and pressed a feather-soft kiss there. My knees felt weak, and I hoped they wouldn't buckle.

"Please tell me how I can help you," he said. "You don't have to go through this alone."

Somehow that did it—that word woke me up, made me snap back to reality. I drew back a bit and finally looked him in the eye.

"I'm not alone," I said, making my voice strong. "I have my sister."

Pain flared in his gorgeous, dark blue eyes. His hands dropped away from me and he stepped back.

I drove home, refusing to cry.

Someone Who Could Help

Outside the airport terminal, Marcel inhaled deeply, then coughed out a lungful of car exhaust. Another thing to long for: the clean, pure air of his home, scented by the sea, by peace. The air in New Orleans had taken a dive since the last time he'd been here.

Still, the moment he'd set foot on the pavement, he'd felt immeasurably better. No longer did he feel as though a thousand insects were crawling under his skin. He'd lost much of his tension, his anxiety—and would lose even more as soon as he saw Daedalus.

The rage, however, would remain.

Here, in the city where virtually every kind of vice was tolerated and condoned, his worn brown monk's robes attracted even more attention than they had in Shannon. He needed help. He had no money, no other clothes. He was completely drained, an emotional shell. It had been days since he'd been able to sleep or eat, thanks to Daedalus.

A taxi pulled up to the curb, and Marcel climbed in. He would go to Petra. She would help him. She always had.

Thais

The next afternoon I eased the Camry into a parking space in front of our house, then forgot to put the clutch in. The engine gagged, then died with a shudder. I winced and turned to Clio, who was wearing her saintly "hope you learn to drive soon" expression.

"Sorry."

"It's okay." Clio gathered her stuff and opened her door. "I'm sure my kidneys will bounce right back."

I laughed. "It wasn't that bad."

"Uh-huh," she said, opening the front gate.

"Isn't all this stuff going to die when it freezes?" I asked, pointing to the plants.

Clio shot me a superior look. "You're such a Yankee."

"It freezes here, right?"

"Every couple of years," Clio admitted. "Let's go see if they finished the back yet."

We'd done as much of the work repairing the back of the house as we could, but Petra had hired professionals to do the rest. Rain had delayed the final paint job, but maybe they'd done it today.

We started down the narrow alley along the side of the house. Without warning, Clio stopped so suddenly that I walked right into her.

"What's—" I began, but her hand motioned me to be quiet. I peered over her shoulder.

"Down there," she barely breathed, and I went on tiptoe to see better.

A brown snake was coiled on the sidewalk right in front of us.

"Is that a good snake?" I whispered.

"It's a copperhead—a water moccasin," Clio whispered back.

"So that's not good?"

She didn't answer. The snake's head swayed as it rose into the air.

"It's going to strike," Clio said without moving her lips. "It's poisonous."

I closed my eyes for a moment, and just like that, words came to me. I breathed them out. "Sister snake, leave us now. Return home to your young. Our place is here. Return and be healthy. *Va-zhee, va, let, monche.*" I didn't know what those last words were, but the snake paused as if it heard me.

It pulled back, as if it were going to leave, but suddenly it swung around. Clio backed up quickly, pushing me behind her, but the snake twisted toward us. Suddenly I remembered my nightmare, the one where the snake was coiled around my neck, choking me.

Clio repeated the spell I'd just said, with the same words at the end. At the last words, she drew two signs in the air, ones I didn't recognize.

Again the snake paused, and again it swiveled back toward us. "Our magick's affecting it, but it's fighting us," Clio said.

I couldn't take the tension anymore. I slid my purse strap off my shoulder and hummed the purse right over Clio's shoulder at the snake. Clio shrieked almost soundlessly and pulled back. My purse hit the snake, and I mentally said, *Sorry, sorry.*

But it did seem to break the snake's concentration. With a last look at us, it turned and slithered under our neighbor's fence so quickly that it was gone in a flash.

I hadn't realized I'd been holding my breath until I let it out with a whoosh.

Clio turned to me. "A snake in our alley."

"Does that ever happen normally?"

She paused, considering. "Well, copperheads *are* all over the place, but not usually uptown. They stay closer to water."

"We're only three blocks from the river," I pointed out. I paused, shivering despite the heat. "Or do you think it was magick?"

"I don't know," Clio said. "I mean, was this an attack?"

She headed toward the back again, and I picked up my purse carefully, looking all around in case the snake came back. I'd lived in Welsford, Connecticut, for seventeen years, and the only dangerous thing that had happened to me had been stepping on a dead bee. Since I'd come to New Orleans, I'd been living in mortal peril, like, every day.

We were almost at the back of the house when we heard Petra's voice and someone else murmuring back to her. The side windows were open over our heads since the house was raised up on brick pilings.

"Are you still worried that she's a dark twin?"

It was Ouida. Once again Clio and I stopped dead. She turned to me, her finger to her lips. *Dark twin?* I thought. *What are they talking about?*

"I'm thinking—" Petra began, but then she stopped. "Are the girls home?"

My eyes widened, and Clio pushed me back down the alley, fast and silently.

"She felt us," she whispered.

"What the heck is a dark twin?" I whispered back.

Clio shrugged, looking clueless. "Your guess is as good as mine." Turning around again, she strode toward the backyard, making sure her feet made noise on the pavement. I followed, still keeping a wary eye out for the snake.

"Yeah, and so I've got to reread that whole section in chemistry," Clio said, pitching her voice just a shade louder than normal. "And I'm so bummed because I already answered all those questions."

I wasn't nearly as good at subterfuge as Clio was. "Yeah," I said, my mind spinning. "Um, I've got lots of homework too. So did they finish painting back here or what?"

Now we were entering the backyard. We walked past the little laundry shed and then "saw" that the back door was open. Inside, Petra was looking out the screen door.

"Hey," I said, waving, hoping my face wasn't too transparent. We hadn't been deliberately eavesdropping, but clearly Petra hadn't wanted us to hear about the dark twin thing. My life was one circle of secrets within another—I was losing count of who knew what and who thought what and who I could maybe trust.

"Hi, girls," said Petra. "Why didn't you come in the front?"

"We wanted to see if they'd finished painting," said Clio. "And it looks like they did."

"Yes, the workmen left a couple of hours ago," said Petra, opening the door. "How was your day? Did you feel safe?"

"Yeah," I said, mounting the steps to the back door. "Until the snake welcoming party when we got home."

"Snake?" Petra looked more amused than alarmed. I dumped my backpack and purse on the kitchen floor. Ouida was sitting at the table, and she smiled and waved a muffin in greeting.

"A copperhead, in the alley." Clio motioned outside with her head, already taking a bite of muffin.

"They're everywhere," said Ouida. "You always hear about people finding them on their car engines or under the fridges."

"What?" I asked in alarm. I looked at our fridge, humming away in the corner.

Petra smiled again. "They like warm places. So they coil up on top of your car engine or under your refrigerator, where the motor is. To be warm."

I didn't know whether to feel relieved that Petra obviously wasn't worried the snake had been another attack on me and Clio or freaked out about the idea that meeting up with snakes was an every-day thing around here. "So, you definitely don't think this was someone trying to go after us again?" I asked, just to be sure.

Petra pursed her lips, thinking. "It's possible, of course, but very unlikely. Since nothing else has happened lately, I would say this was regular old luck that you met that snake."

"Well, either way, can we put an anti-snake charm around the house?" Clio asked. "I hated run-ning into that thing."

"Snakes can be useful," Petra said. "Keeping down the mice and rats."

I sank weakly into a chair. "We have mice and rats now?"

Ouida and Petra both laughed.

"Welcome to New Orleans," Clio said. She looked at me. "Come on, we might as well do our homework upstairs."

I realized she wanted to talk to me alone, so I nodded and grabbed my stuff. My mind was reeling. I had done a spell, without thinking, out in the alley. It had almost worked. Now I wanted to know what a dark twin was. Plus, we had snakes and rats and mice, apparently. Ugh.

In Clio's room, she got out of her sundress and put on high-cut jean shorts and a tight red T-shirt with a silhouette of Bob Marley on it.

"Okay, so what the heck is a 'dark twin'?" I stretched out across her bed.

"I don't know. Ordinarily I'd ask Ouida or Melysa, but I think Nan doesn't want us to know about it." She pulled her hair back into a ponytail and suddenly looked more like me—simpler, less like glamorous Clio. "We should go to the library and check it out or use a computer at Botanika or Café de la Rue."

"Why can't anything be simple?" I groaned. "It seems like I just get used to one thing, and then nine other weird things take its place."

Clio smiled. "Believe it or not, *my* life was much simpler before all this too." She looked up. "Someone's coming."

My first thought was Luc, but it would be crazy for him to come here. He was lying low lately—I hadn't seen or heard about him since Récolte.

The doorbell rang, and Clio went to stand at her open door, listening. We heard Petra walk to the front door and open it.

"Marcel!" she exclaimed, and Clio looked at me with raised eyebrows.

"That's one of the Treize," she whispered. "One that Daedalus got here with his spell of forceful summoning."

"Which one was Marcel?" I came to stand by her. Downstairs we heard murmuring and voices. Petra and Ouida both sounded glad.

Clio frowned, thinking. "Uh—which ones aren't accounted for? He wasn't another slave, was he?"

"I don't remember."

"Wait. No." Clio's face cleared as she remembered. "Oh—Marcel was Cerise's lover, the father of her baby. Cerise wouldn't marry him." She looked solemn.

"Hm. Well, let's go meet him."

We went downstairs—everyone was still in the front room. A young, strawberry blond guy was standing between Petra and Ouida. He was taller than Richard but not as tall as Luc. He had fair skin and blue eyes and looked more Irish than French. He was wearing a brown monk's robe.

When we walked in, he glanced up, then drew in breath with an audible gasp. He actually stepped back and put his hand up, his eyes wide. I wheeled to see if something was behind us.

Oh. It was just us, the miracle twins.

Petra gave a sad smile and took his arm. "Marcel, this is Clio and Thaïs—Clémence's daughters. Girls, this is Marcel Theroux, one of the Treize."

I stepped forward and held out my hand. "Nice to meet you."

The seconds ticked by awkwardly, until Marcel seemed to force himself to touch my hand briefly. "Hello," he murmured, looking down.

"Hi," said Clio, not offering to shake hands. Marcel looked relieved.

"Clio, could you please see if any mint survived in the backyard?" Petra asked her. "I'll make us something soothing to drink. Let's go back into the kitchen."

"We have to get you some new clothes," Ouida said, taking Marcel's arm, almost like he was an invalid, I thought. "Where are you staying?"

"Nowhere," Marcel said faintly. He had a bit of an English? Irish? accent, and I wondered where he'd been and what he'd been doing. Something monk-ish, I gathered. They were walking in front of me, and I happened to glance up as he blocked out the sunlight in the doorway.

This time *I* gasped, stopping in my tracks. His silhouette, the outline of his head and shoulders—he was the man who'd leaned over the dark-haired woman in the vision Clio and I had shared, the day we'd set fire to the house. He had killed someone in the swamp.

They turned to look at me, and I shook my head, looking down. My face flushed. "Saw a spider," I said awkwardly.

"Spiders, snakes—I guess you haven't seen snakes in a while, have you, *cher*?" Petra asked Marcel.

"No," he said.

"Can you come stay with me?" Ouida asked as they sat down at the kitchen table. Clio came in the back door, the strong scent of spearmint preceding her into the room.

"Yes," Marcel murmured, not looking at either me or Clio. "I would appreciate it."

"Have a drink, and then we'll get you settled," Ouida said. "You must be exhausted."

"It was a . . . long journey." His voice sounded tense and sad, as if he were in physical pain. He was very different from the other men in the Treize: pompous Daedalus, quiet but kind Jules, weirdly dark Richard, and then Luc. Marcel seemed even more otherworldly.

And he had killed someone; I'd seen it myself. But Ouida and Petra both seemed to trust him and care about him. I couldn't imagine them feeling that way about someone capable of murder. Yeah, Petra had lied to Clio about huge stuff, and I didn't fully trust *her* to be completely straight with us. But I did believe that the lies she'd told had been to protect Clio and me. She and Ouida were good people at heart. And if they trusted Marcel . . .

Maybe he hadn't really killed that woman in our vision?

I thought about what I had seen. The woman had been facedown in the mud of the swamp. We'd seen someone chasing her—she'd had dark hair and dark eyes, but she'd looked nothing like anyone else we'd met in the Treize. *Think, think.*

Oh my God. Melita, the dark one who had worked the spell—it had been *her*. Marcel had killed *her*. Or had *not* killed her. Everyone in the Treize assumed Melita was gone since she'd never surfaced after that crazy rite so long ago.

But . . . if Melita hadn't died, if she was in fact still alive, then Daedalus wouldn't need both me and Clio for the rite to make a full Treize. I stood frozen in thought, my mind whirling.

What if someone knew that Melita was alive, knew where she was now? They would know that they needed only *one* of us for the rite. Would they be trying to get rid of one of us, then? Maybe they wanted Melita to come back and thought that killing one of us would do it? Which would explain the attacks.

Then again, if Melita was out there, why wouldn't the person who knew it have come forward a long time ago, back when our mom was born, or her mom, or her mom before her. . . . Why wait until twins came along and just get rid of one twin? It seemed pretty far-fetched. Then again, we were talking about a rite that could make people immortal, so I guessed the term *far-fetched* was kind of relative.

All I knew was I had to tell Clio about all of this as soon as I could.

Would That Kill Him?

The taxi glided to a stop. Lying on the backseat, her eyes closed, Claire groaned. She was too tired to get out and deal with this. How much would it cost to just sleep here in the taxi for a while?

"Yo, ma'am, we're here."

The door opened and Claire felt warm air on her legs. With great difficulty she opened her eyes, wincing at the glare. Her driver stood impassively on the sidewalk, no doubt wondering if she would have to haul Claire out herself.

"Okay," Claire managed, struggling upright. She coughed and got out of the cab. Her driver, satisfied that Claire was conscious, popped the trunk and got out Claire's lone, battered suitcase.

On the sidewalk, Claire stretched, breathing in. Noticing the driver looking at her, she rummaged in her purse for American money, which, amazingly, she'd remembered to get at the JFK airport.

She paid the driver, remembering to tip her much more than she'd had to tip anyone in Thailand.

"Thanks, ma'am." The driver got back in the cab and drove off.

Claire stretched again, her short wrinkled skirt riding up, then lit a cigarette, getting her bearings. She looked around. This block of the Quarter hadn't changed much. Some things would be different, she knew, but it had been only about five years since she'd been here. So not too shocking.

She inhaled deeply. At least she didn't feel like she was detoxing anymore, now that she was physically in New Orleans. She had to see Daedalus soon, though, to get rid of the last of the twitching. Bastard. Whatever he'd called her for better be damn important. Yeah, she would go see him. First, though, she needed a bath and a drink and, in the best possible world, both at the same time.

Had anyone ever tried cutting Daedalus's heart out and throwing it into a fire or something? Would that do it? Would that kill him? Because maybe the time had come for someone to try.

Heaving a sigh, Claire put out her cigarette and grasped the handle of her suitcase. One wheel had broken off, and now the suitcase lurched unevenly behind her. She bypassed the big pink house, heading down the crushed-oyster-shell driveway on one side. In the back was a small, long row house, cut into three tiny apartments. Two hundred and fifty years ago, slaves had lived here. Claire shook her head and sighed. You'd think Jules would get over it.

The air was still, as if there were a storm coming. Claire still hated lightning but didn't mind rainstorms too much now. For years after Melita's rite, she'd cringed every time it thundered. But that had been a long time ago.

Pausing for a moment, Claire concentrated, knowing her nerves were jangled. She was desperate for a drink, she was exhausted, her powers were frayed and shot. Yet she was still able to pick up his energy, right here in the first apartment. She climbed the three small steps and rang the doorbell, then pounded on the wooden door. She felt sticky and couldn't wait to get into the bath.

The door opened, and Jules looked out at her without expression.

Claire gave him a big smile and pulled open the screen door. He didn't step aside, so she pushed past him into the dim, cool interior.

"Oh God, that's better," she said, letting her suitcase drop noisily. "It's bright out there." Finally she turned to face him. He was still standing by the door, though he had closed it. She gave him a big smile. "Hi, honey. I'm home!"

Clio

Marcel and Ouida stayed for dinner. He seemed shy and nervous, not big with the smiling. Now Claire was the only member of the Treize we hadn't met. It was so weird, thinking about these people living in a tiny, old-world village together, knowing each other for hundreds of years. Really hard to wrap my mind around.

They stayed up late with Nan, talking, while Thais and I went upstairs.

"I've been dying to talk to you," Thais said when we were brushing our teeth. She waved her toothbrush at me, mouth foaming like a rabid dog. "Number one, I think Marcel is the guy we saw standing over that woman in the swamp, when it looked like he'd killed her. In our vision."

It took me a moment to catch up to her train of thought. But it all came together and I nodded. "You're totally right—I knew he looked familiar, and I couldn't figure it out, but that's it."

"And," Thais continued, "I think that woman was Melita. And no matter how crazy this Melita woman was, does Marcel really seem like a guy who'd murder someone? So what if Melita *wasn't* dead, the way she seemed in our vision and the way everyone else sort of assumes she is? What if she only *looked* dead, but she's really still alive, and someone knows it, then maybe that someone is the someone who's been trying to get rid of just one of us." Thais looked at me expectantly, holding her toothbrush like a wand.

I thought about it. She was right. The woman who had led the rite was the same one we'd seen fall in the swamp. It was also true that all of the attacks had happened to *one* of us at a time, except for the wasps. But maybe that had been aimed at Thais, and I'd only happened to get caught up in it by accident. I nodded slowly.

"Maybe so. But you know, if Melita's out there, then really, wouldn't it make more sense if it's Melita *herself?*" Thais and I stared at each other over the bathroom sink. "Like, she's back for some reason," I went on. "She knows Daedalus is about to do the rite, and she wants to lead it herself. So she's trying to knock off one of us."

It seemed plausible, for about a minute. Then, at the same time, we shook our heads.

"That seems too much, even for this completely screwed-up situation," I admitted. "First of all, we'd have to be right that Melita's even alive, and everyone seems to think she's the one person who managed to actually die after that rite—along with Cerise, obviously. So, she'd have to be alive and just

76

somehow have disappeared off the face of the planet for two hundred and fifty years."

"Then," Thais jumped in, "she'd also have to have come back right at the same time I got here, figuring out that Daedalus wants to do the rite again and thinking she has to get rid of one of us to guarantee her spot. I mean, if she wanted to be a part of the rite before, why wouldn't she have just shown up way earlier?"

"Yeah," I agreed. "I mean, it's possible . . . but it seems pretty out there. Way too many *if*s."

Eyes narrowed, Thais said, "But we have to figure it out."

"We will soon," I promised.

In my room I lay awake, watching the shadows change on the walls. Thoughts careened around my brain like pinballs. By the time I heard Ouida and Marcel leave, felt Nan and Thais drift off into sleep, I was both so tired and so wired that I felt like jumping out of my skin. Finally, I couldn't wait any longer. Still lying in bed, I crafted a sleep spell, sending it out to waft through the house like the scent of a flower. It would coil around Thais and Nan like a comforting blanket, pressing them deeper into sleep, soothing their dreams, quieting any need to get up for a drink of water or anything. It was a lovely little spell that I'd found in one of Nan's old books.

Of course, if Nan or Thais ever found out I'd done it, they'd kill me. Using magick on anyone without their permission was about the biggest no-no there was in our religion. If someone did it to me, I'd want to take them apart. Yet here I was.

I crept downstairs and past Nan's closed door. In the workroom I gathered a few supplies, then let myself out into the darkness of the backyard. It still smelled like ash out here. I wondered how long it would.

Out back, I went into the darkest area, by the brick wall that separated our yard from the empty lot behind us. Nan's compost heap hid me from the house, which felt better, even with the sleep spell.

Quickly and quietly I set up my circle, setting out power stones, filling our four cups, lighting incense. But there was so much on my mind, I kept doing things out of order, kept jumping at the slightest sound, knocked over the cup of water. I thought about seeing Luc yesterday at Botanika and wondered why I'd felt he was Richard, just for a second. And Richard—why had I kissed him, when Luc was the only one I wanted to kiss?

They were both part of the Treize, this new entity that seemed to be taking over my life. Now Marcel was here and Claire probably was too. All of them were here in New Orleans—this city was like a cauldron, and the Treize was going to come to a boil very soon.

I had to be ready for it—which was why I was out here.

I had two goals: to have a protective spell in place for me and Thais and to control the power that the rite would create to make us immortal. Thais and I wouldn't die. I was sure Thais would want it too, once I had convinced her. *Immortal.* Even the word sent shivers down my spine—the very thought of it. Going on forever. Learning more and more. A hundred years, two hundred. I smiled bitterly. Maybe in two hundred years things would work out between me and Luc and Thais. Maybe I could have him for the first hundred, and she could have him for—no.

But I had the magick that would accomplish this.

Finally I had everything in place. I opened the old *grimoire* I'd found at Botanika last night. There was a spell in here that Hermann Parfitte had described as "basic."

Feeling nervous, I reread it and made sure I had set everything up correctly. This was a spell to draw the power of others to you—the first step in learning how to control or subvert that power. I was going to start with smaller creatures, like bugs, and work my way up to humans.

It was both terrifying and darkly thrilling, doing this. It went against everything I had been taught my whole life. It was among the most forbidden magick there was. And certainly, in the wrong hands, it could be evil beyond comprehension.

But I wasn't doing it for evil purposes. I was doing it to protect myself and my family. I was going to learn to do it before Daedalus used it on me— again.

After a last look around at the darkened yard, the windows of the sleeping house, I closed my eyes, let my hands rest on my knees palms up, and concentrated. I let every muscle relax, from the top of my head to my smallest toe. I felt the tiny release of each one, my shoulders, my wrists, my neck. The boundaries between me and magick began to dissolve. I became part of the world, and the world was part of me. I never got tired of that joyful feeling of oneness with everything, where it all made sense, where everything seemed whole and complete and perfect just as it was. I didn't know why it didn't last once I came out of my trance—I only knew that it didn't. In the regular world, colors were paler, sounds more discordant, emotions more jangled.

I began to sing, very, very quietly, almost silently. The spell had been written in French so old I couldn't translate half of it. I was praying there wasn't an unsaid evil purpose beneath the words. I sang the spell and then sang my own song, which contained a whisper of my true name, which put me in context within the world. It called power to me, connected me to the power in all things: tree, rock, air. With my eyes closed, I drew sigils in the air, the ones described in the *grimoire*. This spell was strange in that it didn't specify exactly what creature's powers it would call to you. I assumed it would be insects or perhaps lizards or frogs.

So when I opened my eyes and found six

neighborhood cats and Q-Tip waiting patiently for me, I was shocked. Cats were mammals— higher, very complex beings compared to insects. They surrounded me, watching me even as they washed a paw or followed a wind-shaken leaf.

"Cats," I murmured, amazed. This was *powerful* magick. Q-Tip looked at me, wondering what I wanted. Ordinarily he would have chased strange cats out of the yard, so I knew without a doubt he was under my spell.

The next part of the spell was to access the creatures' power. I was scared—I had no idea what would happen and worried that doing this one spell, taking this one step, would somehow color me evil forever. Like it would take away any hope I had of general goodness. Not goody-two-shoes goodness, which, face it, I'd never had a lot of. But goodness in the sense of . . . lack of real badness.

But the stakes were so high. My life. My sister's life. Would it be better to be tainted dark forever but keep my free will or to be good but controlled by someone else?

I closed my eyes again and murmured the words that would let me access the cats' power. It wasn't gradual, a slow, gentle twining of our spirits. It was sudden, shocking. Within seconds I felt their feline life forces standing all around me, animal sentinels in the darkness. They were alien, totally *other*, not like anything I'd ever felt, even during the wildest circle. Each cat was an unmistakable individual. Their energies were sharp and pointed, little clumps of crackling force; small, wild, and primitive. Even Q-Tip, my baby, who was about as domesticated as they come, felt like: *animal*. It was freaky in the extreme.

Feeling shaken, I went on to step three: joining their energies to mine. I sang the third part of the spell, checking the words again in the *grimoire*, which was open in front of me. I sang the words that let my spirit glide out and encircle theirs one by one, as if I were a stream and they were bits of debris that I was picking up and carrying downstream with me. I sat quietly, feeling the joining. I began to assimilate them—I began to feel catlike.

My eyes popped open. The seven cats were completely still, staring off at nothing. Totally under my power. I had taken their strength, their force, and they were diminished and hollowed because of it. I felt ashamed that I had done this to them. But I also felt an exhilaration: I was super-Clio, more than I had been, more than I had *ever* been. I felt bursting with life and power, and a dark and terrible joy rose up in me. Standing, I held my arms out, trying to encompass this hugeness, this surge of strength.

And then I jumped. The strong feline power within me insisted on showing itself, and without thinking, I coiled my muscles. I crouched and jumped easily to the top of our seven-foot brick wall. Right to the top of it. I landed on my toes, arms out for balance, but felt solid and secure. I could do anything.

Laughing aloud, feeling glorious, I raised my face to the sky. I saw differently, heard differently, tasted the air more powerfully. Every scent the air carried was distinct, clear, strong. The last of the blooming jasmine, the sweet olive, the roses in our neighbor's garden. I smelled other animals, damp brick, green leaves and decaying plants and dirt. Everything tasted exciting, and my senses seemed close to overload. I was giddy with sensation, thrilled, with fierce anticipation about exploring the whole new world opened to me. Laughing, I spun in a surefooted circle on the eight-inch-wide wall. My night vision was amazing, and I gazed at everything, seeing every dark leaf, every swaying plant, every cricket in the grass, one crisp, clear snapshot at a time.

And I saw seven cats, still as stones, on the ground in my backyard.

A sudden fear overtook me, an animal fear, unthinking, strong, violent. *Were they dead?* Had I killed them? If I'd killed them, I'd killed part of me—and worse, I'd become something that filled me with horror. Quickly I jumped down and touched Q-Tip's fur, gleaming whitely in the very slight moonlight. He was alive. Alive, but not himself. And I understood with shame and crushing disappointment what I had done.

I sat down again in my circle, trying to still my frantically beating heart. I didn't *want* to lose this feeling, this incredible, exhilarating extra-ness. It would be so easy to just take it, take it and keep it, and not care about the consequences.

But seventeen years of Nan's teachings and examples were worn into me too deeply, and I was grateful. Her lessons gave me the strength to do what I might not have been able to do on my own. Closing my eyes, I chanted the fourth, last part of the spell, the one that would undo what I had put together. Even before I had finished saying the strange, ancient words, I felt the feline spirits leave me, felt myself becoming less. Less dimensional, less powerful. Flatter, completely human. Our energies flew apart from each other, and each cat came back to life, blinking, looking confused and startled and afraid.

In an instant all the cats scattered. They associated this place with something ill, something they must escape from, and so they ran, slinking under fences, jumping over them, racing down our alley to the street. They were running away from *me* and what I had done.

Except Q-Tip. He sat in front of me, his eyes on mine. He hadn't heard any of the spell, but it had affected him. He was only a cat, but there was an unblinking knowledge in his eyes. He knew what I had done to him. He knew I was the kind of person who would take his power and use it against his will. Slowly he turned away from me and walked to the house, the offended line of his small back seeming a bitter accusation.

"I'm sorry," I whispered. But of course he didn't hear me—none of them did. Guilt and shame crashed down on me. I had taken a lesser being's power and made it my own. And I had loved it so, so much. And I wanted to do it again.

My face crumpled. I tried to hold it in but couldn't—sobs broke out of my chest. I kicked over the candles, the cups of water and sand. Falling to my side, I curled up on the ground and sobbed and sobbed, my arms covering my face, making myself as small as possible. As if I could make myself so small and insignificant that the goddess wouldn't see what I had done, the terrible line I had crossed.

Thais

Melysa was in our house when I got home on Friday.

"Thank God this week has ended." I groaned, dropping my backpack. "Lately it seems like every week takes months and months to get through." I went to the fridge and got some iced tea and a yogurt and sat down at the kitchen table.

"Where's Clio?" Petra said. She glanced out the window, and I realized she was checking the time. I'd become very aware of this lately—whenever Petra or any of the other witches wanted to know the time, they glanced up at the sky first, then sometimes double-checked it against a clock or watch. I couldn't believe figuring out where the sun or moon was could really narrow down the time that much— they were probably constantly late for appointments or TV shows.

"She said she had to run a quick errand. I took the streetcar home." Clio had seemed a little off all day—she'd looked tired and kind of drawn, sad. I'd asked her if she was okay, and she'd said nothing was wrong. I wondered if she was still pining over Luc. I sighed. We'd both loved him so much. And Clio didn't have Kevin to help take her mind off him.

"Did anything happen at school today?"

I felt Petra's blue-gray eyes on me and knew she meant anything weird. I shook my head. "Nope. No snakes, wasps, or streetcar accidents."

Petra shook her head. "I've questioned everybody," she said. "Of course, all of them are terrific liars—we've all had to be over the years. But someone must also be using a spell of concealment."

"The snake might have been just a coincidence," Melysa said. "They're everywhere. I've seen copperheads in the lagoon at City Park. Maybe the attacks really are over."

Petra nodded, looking like she wanted to be convinced. "Maybe so." She smiled at me. "At any rate, I'm always glad when you two get home."

I smiled back and finished my yogurt. I was glad I had a home to come to, no matter how weird it was sometimes. The months I had spent at Axelle's, in the Quarter, had been totally unsettling. Even though Petra and Clio were witches, even though I was now even more caught up in the Treize's drama than before—still, I had a home and people who cared about me. I didn't know if I would ever get over my dad's death. But at least I wasn't floating, lost, in a world I couldn't relate to.

I did my homework at the table while Melysa tied herbs in little bundles to dry. There were racks in the outside laundry room, and now I knew what they were for. Many of Petra's herbs and medicinal plants had been destroyed in the fire, but she'd gathered the ones she could save, and now we had yarrow, skullcap, catnip, lemon verbena, and other plants whose names I hadn't learned yet, all hanging upside down to dry.

Petra was steeping other plants in small copper pots on the stove. She had a whole system where she strained the infusions through cheesecloth into small glass bottles, then stuck preprinted labels on them. These she stored in a cabinet in the workroom. I would never learn everything they knew.

"This stuff I'm going to save till Sunday," I said, closing my chem book. "I got the worst out of the way."

Petra smiled at me. "Clio always leaves everything till the last minute."

"I know. But I hate having it hanging over my head."

Melysa looked up. "Would you like to learn more about a witch's tools?"

I knew about the four cups and the special gowns witches usually wore during circles. Clio had mentioned other tools, but I didn't know much about them. I nodded. "Like what?"

"Well, there's the wand," Melysa said. "You don't have one, do you?"

"No."

"Clio does—why don't you use hers?" Petra

suggested. "I'm sure she wouldn't mind. You won't do enough magick to alter its vibrations very much. I think she keeps it in a box under her bed."

"Okay." I got up and hurried upstairs. A wand. Like Harry Potter! In Clio's room I got on my hands and knees and pushed her bedspread aside. She never made her bed, and the covers always looked like a wrestling match had taken place. An instant image of Clio and Luc together on this bed flashed into my brain, and I literally winced and drew in a breath.

I sat back on my heels and let that breath out. I didn't know if they'd gone to bed or not. I didn't want to know. I thought they probably had—Clio was way ahead of me in that department. I'd never even gotten to third base. But thinking about it, picturing them doing it, was intensely painful, and I'd tried to banish the idea from my mind.

Which I did now.

Another deep breath out, and then I looked under her bed for the box. It was made of inlaid wood and looked very old but well kept. An intricate rose made of several different kinds of wood decorated the top. I pulled it out, and as I did, I noticed the edges of some paper sticking out from between Clio's mattress and her box spring.

I bit my lip. There was no reason I had to know what those papers were. If they were love letters from Luc, I didn't want to see them or even know they existed. If they were Clio's diary, I didn't want to read it.

But I slid my fingers in and pulled it out, as if I were watching someone else do it.

It was a tattered old book, with crumbling pages and a threadbare spine. The cover had been red once, but you could hardly tell anymore. I opened it.

Being the Personal History of One Hermann Parfitte; and How He Learned to Subvert the Power of Others. Oh my God. What was Clio doing with *this*?

I opened the first few pages and skimmed some lines. It was partly in English and partly in French. I saw what looked like spells, but they were in a language I didn't recognize, as if French had been put in a blender. Clio had made some notes in the margins, translated some words. Her handwriting was worse than mine, and I turned the book this way and that, trying to make out what she had written.

A minute later I sat there, quietly freaking. It felt like the pages themselves were sending out tingles of magick. The few words Clio had translated were *control, will, spirit, power, afterlife,* and *living beings.* Oh, jeez. What was this about? Daedalus had taken over our energies at the Récolte circle. Had Clio stolen this from him? Was she trying to learn how to do it herself? Was she trying to figure out how to make herself—and maybe me— immortal? What was she *thinking*? This seemed so dangerous.

I closed the book and pushed it back under her mattress so that none of it was visible—I was betting Petra didn't know about any of this. Clio and I had to talk about it. If she didn't bring it up, I would.

Quickly I opened the box, hoping I wouldn't stumble on any other dark secrets. Thankfully, there were only recognizable tools inside. I took Clio's wand, closed the box, and hurried back downstairs.

Swishing it experimentally, I went back into the kitchen. "Okay, ready," I said.

Not by Ordinary Means

It was still beautiful. Richard turned the knife over and over in his hands, feeling the cool, razor-sharp obsidian edge. The hilt was finely carved and polished to an infinitely black gloss. You could practically see each individual feather strand. He stroked his fingers slowly over the almost-imperceptible ridges, thinking about the last time this knife had been used. Ordinarily it would be impossible to hone an obsidian knife to such sharpness. But of course, this hadn't been made by ordinary means.

Richard uncrossed his legs and rolled his shoulders, stretching out the kinks he had from paddling and digging. The metal box rested on his mattress on the floor. He'd brushed off most of the dirt, enough to see that the metal was untouched by time or rust, the painted symbols still clear and precise. One symbol on the box's lid, black and spiky and flowing, matched exactly the tattoo on his chest, across his breastbone.

There were other things in the box, but just as Richard replaced the knife, the doorbell rang. He frowned, trying to feel who it was, but he couldn't really tell. Someone knocked hard on the door. Shaking his head, Richard slipped the box under a loose floorboard beneath his bed and said a quick spell over it.

The doorbell rang again. The last thing Richard felt like doing was dealing with someone, but it sounded like they weren't going to go away.

He was almost to the door when the doorbell rang *again*.

Richard unlocked the door and pulled it open. "Okay, keep your pants—"

Clio looked back at him, her eyes the clear, deep green of a camellia leaf.

"On," Richard finished. He hated the way his heart sped up when he saw her. What was she doing here in the middle of the day? Or at all? "Aren't you supposed to be in school?"

"It's four o'clock," she said in that superior way of hers, where the "you idiot" was implied at the end. "Is Luc here?"

His eyes narrowed. Just like that, his heart burned, as if someone had tightened barbed wire around it. "Afraid not. Lover boy's out." His voice sounded even and disinterested. Good. He turned and walked down the hall, leaving her. The door shut behind him, but he refused to look back. Then he heard her footsteps, and his throat tightened. For some reason Clio tied him in knots. It was infuriating. No one got to him this way.

His jaw set, Richard went back into his room,

saw his mattress on the floor, and cursed under his breath. *You stupid ass. Why didn't you go to the damn kitchen?* He grabbed his cigarettes and lit one, knowing how much she hated it.

Clio stood in the doorway of his room, seeing it for the first time—the dark blue walls, the painted silver symbols. The room was practically empty except for a low nightstand, the mattress, a small altar in one corner, and a broken dresser.

He turned to look at her, blowing smoke in a stream toward the ceiling. The fan blades chopped it up and it disappeared.

"When will he be back?" Clio asked, her face closed, eyes guarded. She didn't seem to be craving alone time with Richard. Fine. As long as they were on the same page. She was probably still pissed about his grabbing her at Récolte.

"Don't know," Richard said, sounding bored. "I'm not his keeper. Sometimes he stays out all night." Pain and anger flared in her eyes, and Richard felt maliciously pleased. Served her right, mooning over Luc. He'd never had much of a problem with Luc, but somehow this just rankled. He blew more smoke toward the ceiling, keeping his eyes on her.

"Do you have to do that?" she asked tartly. She was standing in the doorway, holding tight to the purse on her shoulder, as if he might mug her.

"It's my room," he told her. "Whatever I want in my room goes."

Clio flicked him a glance, and just like that, the atmosphere between them changed.

Which he wasn't going to mess with. "Go on, then," he said. "Go home."

But she stood there, and for the first time Richard noticed that she didn't look model stunning, like she usually did. There were circles under those green, almond-shaped eyes, and her face looked drawn and tight. She was upset about something. Well, he didn't give a damn. She could stew in her own juices.

"Quit," she said, her voice faltering. Richard just looked at her. "Quit kissing me." She raised her chin a fraction, trying to summon defiance, but instead looking only vulnerable.

Biting down his anger at both her and himself, Richard forced his voice to be neutral. "Fine. You got it. I wouldn't touch you with someone *else's* pole."

For ten seconds—Richard counted—Clio looked at him, emotions crossing her face like clouds across the sky. His cigarette had burned down, and he ground it out in his ashtray. Why wouldn't she go?

She launched herself at him just as he straightened up, and he grabbed her arms in surprise. It wouldn't be the first time an angry woman had come at him, but—

In the next second Clio was holding his head in her hands, kissing him. Richard heard her purse hit the floor.

This is stupid, this is not good, this is not what I should be . . . uhh . . .

His hands slid down her slim, strong arms and held her at the waist. She pressed her lips harder against his so his mouth would open. His brain shorted out and his senses went on overload. She was insistent, molding herself to his body, and then she slid her arms beneath his unbuttoned shirt, her fingers spreading across his back.

He groaned as he felt her heat and urgency, her anger and pain and uncertainty. It was more intoxicating than anything he'd come across so far, and his search had been wide and varied. *Now, now, now.* She pushed her tongue in his mouth and he reciprocated. He wanted her, her wildness. Breaking the kiss for a second, he pulled her down to his bed on the floor, keeping his eyes open so he could see her fine black hair fan across the white sheet. Clio's gaze was locked on his, her face serious and flushed, mouth half open. He gathered her under him. She pushed at his shirt and he helped her get it off, and then her hands were all over him, trailing across his chest and holding him to her and smoothing over his tattoos, leaving heated trails of raw nerves.

He kissed her again, so deeply it was like they had fused together, were drinking from each other. She tasted wild and sweet, not like whiskey, not like cigarettes. Beneath him she was strong and curvy, not tiny, almost as tall as he, and their legs tangled together. Her sandals came off and he pushed them onto the floor.

They shifted onto their sides, still facing each other. Clio kissed him hard on his mouth, his face, his neck. Her teeth bit his neck gently, then she kissed the same place, touching it with her tongue.

Silky hair brushed against his face and he held it back, framing her cheekbones, one thumb touching her birthmark. Goddess, he wanted her, he wanted her more than anyone. . . .

Clio was wearing a thin white shirt over a pink camisole, and he tugged off the shirt easily. Keeping his mouth glued on hers, he slid his hand under her camisole, touching her bare back. Richard couldn't believe this was happening, knew he should stop, knew it was Luc she wanted. But here they were, and she wanted him too.

"Oh. God."

His eyes flashed open to see Clio pulled back, staring at him. Her face was flushed, her lips red and swollen. Inside, his mind was screaming, *Don't stop don't stop don't stop.*

"I thought—I had the thought that I needed to do a nulling spell," she whispered, her voice sounding broken.

Richard blinked as his brain tried to translate her words. Nulling spell. Oh, so she wouldn't get pregnant. Fat chance.

"Good thinking," he got out, reaching for her, but she pulled back, her eyes huge and sober.

"Then I thought—you're with the Treize. You can't have children anyway. But—what are we doing?"

What did she *think* they were doing? He stared up at her, breathing hard, and then it hit him: what the hell were they *doing?*

"We don't even like each other," Clio said,

sounding horrified. She scrambled away from him, one hand at her mouth.

It was like someone had thrown ice water on him. In one *second* the heat and the wanting and the fierce longing to join with her fled, leaving him cold and appalled.

"No, we don't," he said hoarsely. He swallowed. But he'd wanted her so bad. . . .

Sitting up, Richard pushed his hair off his face with both hands, not looking at her. His hair was damp with sweat; his skin felt on fire. With anyone else, he would have spun a string of lies, said anything that would get him where he wanted to go. But the words wouldn't come now—he couldn't do that to her. He got off the bed and leaned against the dresser, a thousand thoughts crashing into his brain. They'd been one zipper tug away from having sex.

"You've never slept with someone you didn't like?" he asked, feeling appalled at what had almost happened.

She moved to sit on the edge of the bed and scooped up her white shirt from the floor. Pulling it on, she lifted her hair out of the collar. Her hair looked like she'd been caught in a tornado.

"No, I have," she said, so quietly he could hardly hear her. "It . . . wasn't anything. It was like . . . eating or taking a bath. Neutral, not bad. But this . . . is way different."

"Yes." No argument there.

"I don't know why. It's too . . ." She shrugged, unable to explain.

"Yeah. But we—really don't like each other," he said, sanity returning like harsh sunlight. "We're just . . . on fire for each other." It was horrible to admit it out loud, but he dared her to deny it.

Frowning, looking unhappy and still flushed, she reached for her strappy sandals and put them on. He tried not to look at her legs, her face, her collarbone, where he'd kissed her so hard she might have a bruise. She seemed completely unlike the arrogant, totally self-assured Clio he'd met, the one he knew could chew up guys and spit them out. Five minutes ago he'd thought he had to have her or die. Now it was like they were both already dead.

Clio stood up, pushing her hair off her shoulders. She reached down for her purse. Richard couldn't go near her.

She hadn't looked at him for several minutes. Now she left without a word, walking down the hall, shutting the front door behind her. All without meeting his eyes.

Despair was nothing new to Richard—it was more of a constant companion. But this gut-turning misery, this twisted yearning, the desire and the horror all mixed up—that was new.

Now that she was gone, Richard lay down on his bed. In a minute he would get up and drink about a half a bottle of scotch. That would be good. Shut his mind down, shut his body down.

The front door opened again and closed. Richard's heart flared—had she come back? If she'd come back, he would take her. No matter what, he would hold her and kiss her and lose himself in her and forget everything but the deep pleasure of not thinking for a while.

"Hey." Luc stood in his doorway. Richard felt like his life had become a surreal movie.

"Hey," he managed, his mind reeling.

"You okay?" Luc frowned at him.

"Yep."

Sighing, Luc leaned against the doorway. "Marcel's here. In town."

Richard's stomach clenched tighter, if that was possible. Perfect. His day was now complete.

"And Claire. She's at Jules's."

"Good." Richard liked Claire.

"You wanna get something to eat?"

Richard thought about it. "Yeah. Give me a minute to grab a shower." A really cold one.

True Love

It was getting darker earlier every day, Sophie thought, hurrying down the street. She'd left her car several blocks away, seizing the first free parking space she'd been able to find. Now she walked quickly away from the river, away from the more touristy parts of the French Quarter, toward the quieter, residential blocks.

Even here in the city, surrounded by lights and noise, one could still notice the changing of the seasons. Sophie thought longingly of the several years she and Manon had spent in northern Virginia. For an almost perfect, storybook balance of seasons, Virginia was the place to go—even better than Paris. Three months of real winter, including actual snow. Three months of glorious spring, the kind of spring that had first inspired the goddess's festivals: a giddy, heady rebirth of life in all forms, painting the earth in a wash of fresh, bright colors. Three months of actual hot summer, hot enough to go swimming in rivers and lakes, hot enough to bask in the sun, feeling languid and soft. Then autumn, the first tingly breezes leaving one's cheeks chilled; the fiery, painted leaves as trees shut down for winter. Apples, leaves crunching underfoot, Récolte and Monvoile celebrations. Each season brought its own particular joys, its own painful beauty. The rhythm and cycle of seasons and time, the yearly death and rebirth that was the basis for the *bonne magie*.

Now she was back in New Orleans, and though the days were growing shorter week by week, still— it was hardly a real autumn.

Sophie crossed a street, easily walking between two cars that were inching toward Canal Street.

New Orleans basically had nine months of summer, then three months of ugly weather. Very few trees lost their leaves, and the ones that did didn't turn gorgeous colors first. Just brown. Then an ugly, wet, usually chilly but sometimes depressingly warm and muggy winter. Then a spring that lasted about a week. Then summer again.

Some of it was beautiful. There was a certain attractive lassitude that came over one after months and months of unrelenting heat. As if keeping up emotional and behavioral standards were too much effort after so many hot months. It broke you through to another place, a place where you acted differently, thought differently, went further and dared more.

Sophie smiled slightly. She'd written a dissertation on this topic in 1983. It was still fascinating to her. She'd shown that to Ouida, hadn't she? Ouida would probably enjoy it.

Looking up, Sophie saw the big pink house, the

address that she remembered. There was a crushed-oyster-shell driveway on the right side, and she walked down it. Jules could afford any place he wanted—they all could. After two hundred years, even the most imprudent of investments paid off. All of them were well-off, never needed to work again. Experience had shown most of them that lack of purpose led to madness. They needed occupations, jobs, interests, responsibilities to keep sane.

She wished Richard would admit that, get his life together. And Luc.

Her lips pressed together for a moment, then she shook her head. This was it, the first apartment. She rang the bell, feeling Jules within. He answered the door and smiled when he saw her.

"*Salut*, Jule" she said, leaving the *s* off his name.

"Come in, *petite*," he said, holding the door open.

Inside it was dim—the windows faced east, and the sun was setting. The furniture was mismatched, but everything was severely tidy and well cared for.

"Something to drink? Sherry?"

"Oh yes, please. Lovely." Sophie sat on one of the couches, feeling herself relax for the first time in days. Axelle probably hadn't talked to Jules—she seemed to think Jules's loyalty to Daedalus would overrule his judgment. Sophie wasn't sure of that.

Jules came back with two small, delicate glasses of sherry. Sophie inhaled its scent, warm, a bit woody, rich. She took a sip and let it trickle down her throat.

"I wanted to talk to you," she said, loving the

103

honest warmth of his eyes. "Have you been thinking about what—"

The slamming of the back screen door interrupted her. Sophie's eyes widened as Claire came through the back bedroom and the kitchen to the front room. Daedalus's summoning spell had worked. Of course. And Claire was staying with Jules. This was awkward.

"Well, hello, Sophie," said Claire. She was wearing Hawaiian-print capris and a red spaghetti-strap top. Plastic flip-flops with big red flowers over the toes seemed to glow against the floor's dark, scarred wood.

"Hello, Claire," Sophie said politely. Her mission would have to wait till another time. Claire's green eyes were sharp, taking in Sophie from head to foot.

Sophie waited, wishing she had never come, though of course she'd have had to see Claire sometime. Claire was one of them, just like Sophie. One of the Treize. She and Claire hadn't gotten along since Sophie was eight and Claire was nine. Even then they had been the antithesis of each other, and almost two hundred and fifty years had done nothing to change that.

"Why, you haven't aged a day," Claire said, smirking. She sat down in a rocking chair across from the sofa.

Unfortunately, neither have you, Sophie thought, giving a tiny smile at Claire's tired joke.

"Whatcha got there? Sherry? How about a little *coupe* for me, eh, Jules?"

Getting up, Jules went to the tiny galley kitchen.

104

Sophie took a sip, trying to finish her drink quickly so she could leave.

"I hear you're still with Manon."

Sophie looked up. "Yes," she said warily.

Claire leaned back in the rocking chair, looking at the ceiling. She gathered her wild magenta hair in both hands, twisting it into a ponytail. "Well, good for you," she said.

Sophie waited, but Claire didn't sound sarcastic.

"I guess it's true love," Claire went on. "If I ever found true love, I'd stay with it too." She glanced at Jules, but he wasn't looking at her. He poured some burgundy liquid into a small glass and brought it to her.

"Thanks, babe," said Claire. She turned back to Sophie. "Manon got a tough ride. Her and Richard— their situations suck. But it's good, you with Manon. You seem good together."

Sophie nodded, wondering how sincere Claire was being. This was the most personal they had ever gotten, except for an ugly fight back in 1931.

"I'm going to see Richard later, I think." Claire took a big sip, emptying almost half her glass. "Him and Luc. I guess they're batching it, more or less, over on Ursulines."

"Yes." Sophie finished her drink with relief and stood up. "Thank you, Jules—I'll call you later. Nice to see you again, Claire. I'm sure we'll all be getting together again soon—whether we want to or not."

Claire laughed, sounding bitter. "What do you think of Daedalus's scheme, Sophie?"

It was a direct question, one that many members of the Treize had skirted but not voiced.

Shrugging, Sophie edged toward the door. "I need to think about it some more," she said. "I don't know how much he's worked out, and I need to know more about what's going to happen."

Jules nodded at her—they could talk about it later.

"Thanks." Sophie opened the door. The sun had just set, and there was a magickal sensation in the air, the everyday magick of day turning into night. She headed out into it, retracing her steps back to her car. That visit had been a complete bust.

Then she realized, if Claire were here, Marcel probably was too. Sophie grimaced at the thought of Marcel. She didn't want to see him. It would be lovely if she never had to see him again.

No Room for Her

Divination was one of Daedalus's least-favorite disciplines. It was imprecise at best, positively misleading at worst. And not a fun way to spend a Saturday morning, either, in his opinion. He'd wanted Jules to help him with this spell, but Jules hadn't answered his phone this morning. Of course, with Claire staying with him, they might have been out, or perhaps Claire had unplugged the phone.

Daedalus's lip curled with disdain. If he could possibly have done without Claire, he would have, in a heartbeat. He had no idea what Melita had seen in her, what purpose she had served. In the centuries since, she'd proved to be as useless and weak as she'd seemed in their village. Now he was shackled to her for all time and was even in the nauseating position of being dependent on her, needing her, for his rite.

Yet another thing Melita had to answer for. Admittedly, one of the smaller issues.

Now Daedalus made a circle on the wooden floor. Axelle was out—perhaps she had joined Claire and some of the other dissolutes Daedalus was saddled with. Richard, Luc. . . . He was fond of Richard but had no illusions about him. Of all of the Treize, Richard was probably the least moral, the least mindful of the subtle differences between right and wrong. Luc cared but was compelled to choose wrongly again and again, then was tortured about it. Axelle was easily swayed, easily led, content to do whatever served her best, as long as it wasn't too inconvenient.

Working calmly and efficiently, Daedalus set up the rest of the spell. It was one he had performed countless times over the decades, always without result. But now—now things might be different. He felt it. He felt that there were signs all around him, telling him that now was the time.

Daedalus's element was air. He set up five thin sticks of incense in a wooden holder and lit them. Their coiling streams of smoke twined together, weaving a rope of scent. Daedalus began chanting softly, letting himself drift into concentration. This was the hardest part: the releasing of self to merge with and access the world of magick. Daedalus hated the feeling of vulnerability, of letting down his walls. True, it was only moments before that vulnerability was replaced by a surge of power—still, it had never gotten easier.

He forced himself to sit quietly, to release his mild irritation at Jules not being home, his disapproval that Axelle had stayed out all night, his disappointment that so few of the Treize had lived up to his hopes or expectations. One by one he set these thoughts free, like balloons floating away into the atmosphere.

His gaze shifted out of focus as he became aware of his connection to magick. It was there; it was always there for the taking. As usual, it caused an unstoppable flood of joy within him, almost embarrassing in its strength and the eagerness with which he embraced it.

Unseeing, tracing the symbols by memory in the air before him, Daedalus wrote the runes *ôte*, for birthright, inheritance; *deige*, for clarity, awakening; *is*, for obstacle, something frozen or delayed. Then he wrote the sigil for things revealed, veils dropped, and another sigil to enhance the sensitivity of his vision.

Then he waited. *Inhale, exhale.* The beating of his heart. *Don't search; let it be revealed.*

The smoke formed a thin, hazy curtain in front of him. He watched, trying to divorce himself from want, trying to just be, with no expectations. Which was almost impossible for him, even after two centuries' practice.

But there—there. In the smoke, the haze, an image was forming. A face. Black eyes, straight nose, generous mouth. A woman, not a girl. She was laughing.

Is this what I need to see? The image seemed to realize he was there. Its expression froze, looking surprised. Then it was gone, as if a wind had swept it away.

Daedalus blinked and shook his head.

He'd done that spell what—thirty times? Fifty? Seventy? He'd never gotten an image before. He wasn't great at scrying—he found it hard to believe stories people told about seeing this, that, and the other thing. Only a few times had he received useful or pertinent information. So this was hard to take at face value.

Melita's face, that was.

If he believed it, then she truly was nearby, after all this time. She wasn't dead. He'd been searching for her for so long—could this be real? *Was* she nearby? Was she aware of what he was doing?

Lost in thought, Daedalus automatically cleaned up evidence of his spell. He hadn't heard Axelle come home, but he cast his senses to make sure. No—no one was here but him. He put away the incense, the chalk, the stones.

Melita. If she were back, it would be either truly remarkable or truly, truly disastrous.

She Can't Hide It

The woman behind the counter looked at Luc, then down at the collection of ingredients he was buying.

"Dove feathers, honey, dried foxglove," she murmured. Her squarish brown hand turned a small green glass bottle so she could read its label. "Dried snakeskin."

Luc kept his face impassive.

She met his gaze, as if weighing the light and the dark within him. He tried not to breathe a sigh of relief as she rang up the items and put them in a small paper bag. He paid and slipped the bag into his leather sack.

"Thanks," he said.

"Do you—" the clerk said, making him pause. "Are you sure you be wantin' these things, now?" Her voice was warm, her brown eyes knowing. She had a slight, singsongy Jamaican accent.

"Yes," Luc said briefly.

"Do you be careful, then, man," she said solemnly.

"Yes," he said again, and left.

It seemed like decades ago that Clio had taken him here. Luc leaned against the broad trunk of the live-oak tree, looking down into the cradle formed by its thick roots. He and Clio had lain together in this hollow, hidden from passersby.

Now he stepped over the roots and set his small leather sack on the ground. He wished he were in . . . Africa. Or somewhere far away. Where he wouldn't have to deal with Daedalus or any of the Treize.

Then Daedalus would just summon him by force. He grimaced. Claire was doing a burn, no doubt about it. She'd spent most of last night fantasizing about ways to kill Daedalus. It had been pretty funny. But goddess, her and Richard together—they were both so bitter and hard. It got to be too much after a while. Of course they all had cause to be that way. But after hours of eating and drinking with those two, Luc had felt like he'd been dipped in acid and rubbed with sandpaper. It had been a relief to leave them.

Luc heard voices. Probably students from Loyola or Tulane. He lay down, sinking onto the warm, dry earth. Someone would have to be practically on top of him to see him now. On his back, he looked up through the leaves at jigsaw pieces of cloudy sky.

Clio. Clio and Thais. As usual, the thought of Thais made his jaw clench and his gut ache. Her sweetness, her acceptance. He was dully surprised that she was still so angry, so hard against him. At Récolte, she'd been cold and unyielding—at least, until they were in the middle of that awful circle, their emotions being ripped out of them and used as fodder. He'd felt her then. Felt the deep and powerful love she had for him. He'd felt her anguish, her

112

anger. And her love. She was much stronger than he would have thought possible.

Now she was seeing that boy, that stupid boy, kissing him, wrapping her arms around him. If Luc were dark, really, truly dark, no holds barred—that boy would have had a car wreck by now.

Good thing he wasn't that dark.

Sitting up, Luc unpacked his supplies. With a stick he drew a circle in the dirt around him and set four stones at the four compass points. This was dark enough. This was sinking to new lows, even for him. Already he was going further than he'd thought he'd have to. Ten years ago—five—none of this would have bothered him. But there was something about the twins—a vulnerability coupled with an incredibly compelling strength. He hadn't felt so strongly about anyone in—ever? He frowned, trying to remember. He'd loved Ouida, in his way. He'd loved other women over the years, the centuries. But who had *gotten* to him this way? Who had ever caused this deep hunger in him? Had anyone? He couldn't recall.

It was almost sunset. Luc sat in the middle of his circle, closed his eyes, and let himself sink into a trance. *Leaf of tree, cloud of sky, come to me and know not why. I draw you here, with blood and bone. I know you're near, Clio, my own.*

There. He sent it out into the world, feeling it leave him, aiming straight and true toward the one he called. Similar to what Daedalus had done but on a much smaller scale: if Clio were even fifty miles away, she wouldn't feel it. Daedalus's call had reached to the other side of the world. Also, Clio could resist this one if she wanted to, if she was strong enough. Not by just shrugging it off—she'd have to work a little. But she could do it. He wondered if she would.

The sun had almost completely set by the time he had his answer.

He felt her before he heard or saw her, felt her angry energy. But she had come.

When she was close, he opened his eyes. She was striding toward him, her face set in a grim expression.

"How dare you!" she practically spit at him when she was close enough. He had the sudden thought that if he'd been standing up, she would have punched him. As it was, she swung her woven straw purse and smacked him on the head.

"Ow!" It hurt but was so unexpected he almost laughed.

"You used a *spell* on me!" she snapped furiously. "A week ago, you punched Daedalus out for doing the same thing to you! You hypocrite!" She actually kicked him, but she was wearing soft-soled beaded ballet slippers, so it probably hurt her more than him.

He stood quickly, holding up his hands. "Yes, yes," he said, speaking softly. "I'm sorry. You're right, it was a terrible thing to do—"

"*Another* terrible thing to do," she said, her green eyes narrowed. "You just seem to keep coming out with them, don't you?"

"I'm sorry," Luc said again. "I was desperate—I had to see you, talk to you. I'm sorry I used a spell, but I didn't know what else to do. Clio, please, please, just sit and talk to me for a minute. Please."

She crossed her arms over her chest, pressing her breasts upward against her olive green camisole top. A couple of circuits in Luc's brain threatened to short out, but he ruthlessly damped them down.

"You have one minute," Clio said, her voice like an arctic wind.

"Okay, all right." Luc ran one hand through his hair. He'd rehearsed this speech so many times, but as usual, seeing Clio in person made all his thoughts go haywire. "I . . . miss you."

Clio's perfect upper lip curled in a sneer.

"Clio—I screwed up. I'm sorry. I hurt you and Thais both, and I can't ask for forgiveness. It was inexcusable."

She didn't contradict him.

"But I miss you," he said, forcing the words out. Not that they weren't true—they were. But he hated feeling so exposed. "I'm not . . . a bad person. I'm just someone who's been around too long, seen too much, done too much." He shook his head, feeling bleak. "You made me feel new again. Like . . . everything was new. New and exciting because I was sharing it with you. You brought life into my world. And I destroyed it."

Clio waited.

"For the last two hundred and fifty years, I just wanted time to speed by, to hurry up in case I could

115

finally have a chance to die. When Daedalus approached me, he said I could use the power of the rite any way I wanted. I could get more power, change the course of my magick—or die. I wanted to die, to end this pointless, endless existence." He looked up. Clio's face was calmer, and she was watching him with alert interest. He felt the slightest stirring of hope.

"Then I met you. You changed my world, changed how I felt. Stupidly, I destroyed it. When I met Thais, it was like . . . she was the part of you that you were holding back. And you were the part of her that she doesn't let go. I wasn't thinking, wasn't using my head. It was just, my heart told me to try to have every aspect of you."

Those green eyes narrowed. Not good.

He shrugged, hopeless again. "I'm sorry. I've said it was stupid, and it was. I was overwhelmed, I was out of my league, and I made a huge, hurtful mistake. You've told me what you think of me, that you never want to see me again. And if it were anyone but you, Clio, I would take you at your word and leave. Not bother you anymore."

He wished she would sit down. He wished he could touch her.

"But you're too important," he went on. "In more than two hundred years, you're the one who stands out, who my heart yearns for. You've had too much of an impact on me. Anyone who's reached me the way you have—I have to pursue. Don't you see? *Letting* you go would be an even bigger mistake than making you want to go in the first place."

They were standing within a triangle of three enormous live oaks. It was almost completely dark; minutes had passed since Luc had been aware of anyone passing by. Clio was leaning against a tree trunk, arms still crossed over her chest. She didn't say anything, and her face was closed, not giving away her thoughts.

"I'm not asking you to love me again," he said, with a bitter, self-deprecating laugh. "I'm not asking you to even *like* me. I'm asking you to let me love *you*, even if from a distance. Let me care about you. Let me try to make it up to you. I *can* be loyal. I *can* be true. I *can* make you happy. Please let me."

Now he saw indecision flicker in her eyes.

"And where does this leave Thais?" she said coolly, her tone not matching her expression. "Out in the rain? She was stupid enough to care about you—I think *she* actually loved you." The words were snide, meant to hurt, and they did. But he couldn't let himself think about Thais now. If he did, everything would be lost.

Luc bit the inside of his lip and nodded, determined to take whatever she dished out.

"Thais has recovered, it seems," he said stiffly.

Clio scoffed. "Kevin? God, you're an idiot."

Luc met her eyes. "I care about Thais," he said honestly. "I'm appalled and horrified at how I hurt her—and you. I met you first, Clio."

Several emotions passed across her eyes as she looked at him. Then she pushed off from her tree. "I have to go," she said flatly.

117

In a split second, Luc reached out and took one of her hands, pulling her gently back. She would kill him if he tried to kiss her mouth, but instead he pressed his lips against her warm, soft palm. A flare of passion seared him, almost making him pull back in surprise. Clio wasn't as aloof as she seemed. There was still strong feeling between them.

He stood up, searching her face. She looked upset, still angry, but also torn with longing.

Pulling her hand away from him, she strode away over the dark grass, not looking back.

Thank the goddess I
hadn't driven, I thought as I slammed through our
front gate. I would have wrecked the car, I was so
furious. I'd thought I was losing my mind earlier—
one minute I was standing in the kitchen, washing
dishes, and the next I was practically shrieking with
the need to see Luc immediately. Then I'd had the
image of him waiting in the park, just a few blocks
away.

I'd almost gasped with shock. *He'd put a spell on me.*

And the truth was, I still loved him. Still longed
for him. It had taken everything I had to resist him.
Here's the sick part: I almost wished he had put a
spell on me to make me give in, so I could just do it
and not blame myself for being stupid and weak and
betraying Thais. I was pathetic.

Opening the front door, I was greeted by air only
slightly cooler than outside. Nan hated air-condi-
tioning, and even when she ran it to dry the house
out so we wouldn't have mold and mildew everywhere, it still wasn't the frigid blast I wanted. I
headed upstairs, deciding to stand under a cold

shower for a long time. I heard Nan's radio playing in the kitchen and figured she and Thais were still cleaning up after dinner. Thais had a date with the Kevster.

I wished she were really in love with him. If she were, if she had really moved on from Luc, then maybe—

"Hey."

I started, not expecting to see Thais sitting on my bed. Had she felt Luc's summoning spell too?

"Hey," I said, putting down my purse and pushing off my shoes. I was glad I had kicked Luc. I should have done it harder. I released a tight breath, hoping I appeared somewhat normal. "Here for a pre-date fashion consultation?"

I scooped my hair up in both hands and secured it with a clip, trying to look bright and chipper, but Thais was watching me with a serious expression on my face. Our face. "What," I said.

"So, whose energy do you want to subvert?"

In books they always talk about how "the blood drained out of her face" or whatever. But this time I *actually felt* the blood draining out of my face, leaving me cold and clammy. This was so far from what I'd been expecting that I suddenly needed to sit down in my desk chair. Oh goddess, I could be in such huge trouble.

"What do you mean?"

She gave me a "please" look. "I mean, why do you have that book hidden under your mattress? What are you doing with it?"

I looked at her, trying to decide the best course of action. Denying everything seemed to be out. All the scary, dismayed feelings from the night I'd worked the spell on the cats came back to me, and I really didn't want to talk about it.

But.

This was my sister. Was it true, what Luc (the bastard) had said to me, that together Thais and I made up one whole? Was Thais everything about myself that I suppressed and vice versa?

"Well," I began. Then it all crashed down on me at once: seeing Luc just now, practically having *sex* with Richard just *yesterday*, the spell with the cats . . . I felt tears well up in my eyes and blinked them back.

"Clio," Thais said softly. "Just tell me what's going on."

"You can't tell Nan." I felt totally bleak.

"Yeah, okay."

Blinking back more tears, I looked at her. "It's . . . important. This is between you and me."

Thais smiled at me, and it was so weird—it was a really old, *wise* smile. For just a second she wasn't Thais at all but someone different, someone much older. I blinked again and she looked just like herself. I must have imagined it.

"*Everything* is between you and me," she said.

I nodded and let out a couple of breaths. "I bought that book," I said, so low I could hardly hear it myself. "From the restricted area at Botanika."

"Why?"

"I'm curious," I said. "Daedalus was able to take our power at Récolte. I wanted to know how." I opened my mouth to tell Thais about trying that spell and being so horrified at what I'd done to all the cats. What a relief, to blurt it out, to tell my twin everything. But it was like a train coming to a junction—I meant to take one path, but the tracks switched and suddenly I was on a different path.

"I thought if I knew how he'd done it, I could figure out a way to stop him from doing it to us again." Perfectly true.

Thais frowned, looking out my window at the top of the mimosa tree in the front yard. Its leaves were just starting to turn yellow, and they shone under the reflection of the streetlight. Soon they would fall off. It was one of the few trees that changed with the seasons.

"Is this about Récolte or the other rite?"

"Both."

"Are you learning how to become immortal? Is that it?"

"Well . . ." I hesitated. I had to convince her. But something told me if I blurted it all out now, she would be turned off and wouldn't go for it. "Not really. More about how to control power once you have it. So no matter what happens with this rite or any rite, no one can use us like that again. I want to make sure you and I are safe from whatever these freaks try to do next."

"So have you learned anything? Have you tried any of the spells?"

"No." I shook my head, feeling so tired. I grabbed a tissue and blew my nose. "I mean, yes, I'm sort of learning stuff, but no, I haven't tried any of the spells."

"Are you learning how Daedalus got our power at Récolte?"

"I don't know," I said slowly. "Sometimes I just don't understand it—it doesn't make sense. I can't see how something would work. But I just got the book a few days ago, and I haven't been able to spend a lot of time on it. I just wanted to, you know, learn about it."

Thais nodded, then glanced at the watch on her wrist. "I want to talk about this more," she said. "But I have to get ready—going to a movie with Kevin. Listen, tomorrow or some time when we're both free, let's go over everything together, okay? Maybe it'll seem clearer if we just hash it all out."

"Yeah, that would be good." What else could I say? "Are you going to wear that?" I asked, just as her mouth opened.

She glanced down. "No. I'm going to put on a sundress. With a sweater, in case the movie's cold."

"Do you have a cute sundress?" I asked, raising one eyebrow skeptically.

"Yes." Her chin lifted a fraction.

"No, I mean a *cute* sundress."

Sighing, Thais stood up and opened my closet doors.

There was nothing good on TV, as usual. It was unbelievable to me that popular Clio was home alone on a Saturday night while wallflower Thais had a date with a really cute guy. The more I moped around the house, the more I felt myself weaken about Luc. I could call him. I could see him. Thais wouldn't have to find out.

It felt horrible.

Time to go to Racey's. Luckily, she didn't have a date either. How the mighty had fallen. But Della and Kris and a couple of others would be there, and we were going to eat junk food and listen to music and do something girly, like paint our toenails. It would be distracting, which was what I needed.

"Okay, later, Nan," I said, popping my head into the kitchen.

"You're going to Racey's?" she asked, marking her place in her book.

"Uh-huh."

"Be careful," she said. "Don't be too late, okay? You have your phone?"

"Okay, okay, and yes." I grabbed an apple from the bowl on the kitchen table and took a big bite. Nan smiled at me, and I smiled back as I grabbed the car keys, then quickly looked away. It was still hard sometimes, being alone with her and acting like things were fine, normal, when they weren't and I didn't know if they ever could be again between us. She'd lied to me for seventeen years. She'd had her reasons, yeah, but those reasons had kept me from ever meeting my own father.

I took a deep breath as I walked outside, forcing it out of my head. It hurt so much, but there wasn't anything I could do to change it. I had to focus on the things I could control.

The Camry was right outside. I cranked the windows open to get the heat out. When would it cool off? November? December? Ugh. I took another bite of apple and left it in my mouth as I pulled away from the curb. Good thing Luc couldn't see me now—no makeup, hair in a sloppy clip, and the crowning touch, an apple stuck in my mouth. Lovely.

What was Luc doing? Was he just yanking my chain? I thought so, but then, he seemed so serious, so sincere. *Right*, I thought sarcastically. *And his sincerity means so much.*

And then Richard. What was I doing *there*? Why did he have that effect on me? I couldn't stand him—but every time I saw him, I wanted to knock him down and rip off his shirt.

At St. Charles Avenue, I took a right, and the steering wheel grabbed a little bit, almost locking up. Surprised, I yanked it hard and made the turn. Should I pull over? Was something wrong?

I glanced down at the dashboard and felt my breath sucked right out of me. The temperature gauge was as high as it could go, and I'd only gone about eight blocks!

I looked around the street, searching frantically for somewhere to pull over, but there were parked cars everywhere. Adrenaline flooded my veins as I scanned for someplace to stop. Suddenly actual flames and smoke erupted from beneath the car's hood, and cars started blaring their horns at me. At the very next corner I wrenched the steering wheel as hard as I could, making a wide and clumsy turn off St. Charles. As soon as I was close to the curb, I jerked the keys out, grabbed my purse, and jumped out of the car.

My hands shook as I fumbled for my cell phone to call for help, running across the street.

A loud *whoosh* noise erupted behind me and I turned and stared as flames completely engulfed my car. This was impossible. I'd had the Camry serviced three weeks ago, and they'd checked everything.

Numbly I started to dial 911, then heard sirens already screaming closer. I remembered that the car had a frigging *gas tank* and rushed away, running halfway down the block. The first fire engine wheeled around the corner as tears started streaking down my cheeks. My car. How had this happened? Had I fried the radiator?

Or.

Was this an attack? I still thought the snake might have been—it had seemed to resist our magick. Maybe this was a follow-up.

Thirty yards away, the firefighters connected a hose to a hydrant and flooded my car. I started weeping in earnest, like a total crybaby. Clouds of white steam and black smoke billowed into the night sky, obliterating stars. A small crowd had already gathered, and now a firefighter was striding toward me.

"Miss? Is that your car?"

I nodded, wiping my eyes and getting to my feet.

"I don't know what happened," I said, trying to pull myself together. "I was driving, and then the steering wheel felt funny, and then I noticed that the temp gauge was way high, and then boom, the whole car was in flames." More tears rolled down my cheeks, and I wiped them off with my sleeve.

"Had you filled the radiator recently?"

I nodded. "Just three weeks ago. And I'd only gone eight blocks! How could it overheat so fast?"

The firefighter shook his head. "I don't know, miss. Your insurance company will check it out. A tow truck is on its way to take it to a car shop—but you know it's totaled."

"Uh-huh," I said brokenly, leaking more tears.

"Do you have someone to call?"

"My . . . grandmother." When Nan got here, maybe she would be able to tell if someone had tampered with the car.

It was now official: every single aspect of my life was dark, negative. I didn't feel good or happy about *anything*, not like I used to. It was like I wasn't even me anymore.

Two Black Sheep

The Napoleon House was packed, since it was Saturday. Frowning, Luc pushed through the crowd and debated whether it was worth it to wait for a table or even a spot at the bar. The smell of warm muffalettas reached his nose. Maybe he should wait.

"Luc!"

Luc turned to see Richard and Claire sharing a table at the edge of the courtyard. Richard raised a tall glass of beer at him, and Luc walked over.

"Hello, tall, dark, and immortal," Claire said, grinning. She took a gulp of a frozen piña colada and waved him to a seat. "Sit down. You hungry?"

"Yeah." Luc caught the eye of a waiter and ordered a scotch straight up and half a muffaletta. "So, what are you two up to tonight?"

"Drinkin'. Eatin'," said Claire. "You?"

Luc shrugged. *Putting a spell on Clio* would probably make them laugh, but he didn't want it getting around.

"So give me your take on the old crackpot's scheme," Claire said. She finished her drink and ordered another when the waiter brought Luc's food.

Again Luc shrugged. "The problem is, he's not a total crackpot. He wants power, and he knows how to get it. He's willing to run us all down doing it."

Claire nodded, mulling it over, and Luc saw the shrewd intelligence in her eyes. It was so easy to forget how smart she was, how sharp. "How many of us are on board with the rite?"

"Axelle, Jules," said Richard. He lit a cigarette and blew the smoke upward. "Me, Manon. Possibly Ouida. Possibly Petra. Possibly Sophie."

Claire looked at Luc. *"Et tu?"*

"On board," he said, taking a bite of his enormous sandwich. Warm cheese, spicy salami, olive salad, Italian bread—it was damn near perfect.

"Interesting," said Claire.

"What about you?" Richard asked.

"On board, I believe," she said, sounding coy. "Trying to come up with a Christmas list."

Richard laughed dryly. "Aren't we all?"

"Tell me about these surprise twins of Petra's." Claire bummed one of Richard's cigarettes and lit it, the smoke obscuring her face for a second.

There was silence, and Luc felt Richard's dark eyes on him.

"They're the latest in Cerise's line," he said slowly, pushing some olive salad back under the bread. "The thirteenth generation. Apparently Petra helped their mother have them, and when she saw it was twins, she took one and didn't tell the father. So one grew

129

up with the father, in Connecticut, and one of them grew up here, with Petra."

"Petra wanted them apart," Claire said. "Did she already suspect Daedalus of wanting a complete Treize?"

"Don't know," Luc said. "She just thought the two together wouldn't be safe, for some reason. Then their dad died this summer."

"We think Daedalus, and probably Jules and Axelle, killed him," Richard put in matter-of-factly.

"Jules wouldn't do that," Claire said, somewhat sharply.

Richard raised his eyebrows. "Jules has followed Daedalus for years. And he might very well have plans of his own too. Together they wrangled it so Axelle got custody of the northern twin."

"Thaïs," Luc murmured, and felt Richard looking at him again.

Claire laughed. "Yeah, 'cause Axelle has always had maternal yearnings. That's hysterical."

Luc couldn't help smiling, and so did Richard.

"Yeah," Luc said. "So Axelle brought Thaïs here. Bizarrely, she and Clio ended up going to the same school, ran into each other, and figured everything out."

"That's the abbreviated version," Richard said, taking a drink of his own scotch.

"Really," Claire said, alert and interested. "What's the long version?"

"Yes, Luc," said Richard. "Tell Claire the long version."

Luc shot him a look. "Not much to tell."

Richard laughed and Luc narrowed his eyes at him, aware that Claire was following this exchange.

"And then at Récolte, Daedalus seized our power and summoned you and Marcel," Luc went on, skipping several chapters. "And now we're all waiting to see how it plays out."

"Mm," said Claire.

Luc could practically see the gears in her head turning.

"And while we're all waiting, Petra has the twins." Claire took the piece of pineapple out of her drink and bit into it. "And the rest of the Treize are fermenting in the cauldron of New Orleans, eh? No one's worried about the twins? No one's trying to keep them separate?"

"Worried? Well, Petra made everyone promise that they would leave the twins alone," Luc said.

"Too late." Richard smiled sardonically into his glass. He was really getting under Luc's skin. He hoped this wouldn't turn into a bar fight in the middle of the Napoleon House.

"Why would they be keeping them separate?" Luc asked, trying to keep his anger down. "I never understood why Petra separated them in the first place. I mean, the whole twin-power thing is just a myth, right?"

"Luc." Claire's eyes, green but nothing like the twins', were quietly amused. "Of course it's not a myth. I can't believe Petra's being so reckless, having them together. Thank God the northern one doesn't know magick yet. The two of them doing magick together could blow you, me, and Daedalus right out of the water."

"But . . . they wouldn't," Luc said, surprised. "They're not . . . dark."

"They don't need to be," Claire said. She held the head of a crawfish up to her bright red mouth and sucked the juices out of it. "They don't need to be dark or light or to know what the hell they're doing. They only have to be together. Did you sleep through this part of the *famille histoire*?"

"They're dangerous?" Luc just couldn't take it in. "How? Why?"

"Because they're twins, they're the thirteenth generation, they're marked—I mean, hello. What part of 'disastrous prophecy' do you not understand?" Claire drained her latest drink and shook her magenta hair off her shoulders.

"What's this prophecy say again?" Richard asked. He seemed weird, tightly wound, angry, worried— Luc couldn't put a finger on it.

Claire slowly ran a finger around the top of her glass, making an annoying, high-pitched hum. "The marked girl brings you death," she said. Then, laughing, she shrugged. "They will bring eternal life and also death. The Twin Angels. You know. The Twin Angels of Life and Death."

"Angels, yeah," Richard muttered. His eyes were glazed. Drunk off his ass, Luc thought. And in a weird mood. Time to get out of here. Richard drunk and in a bad mood meant that blood was going to be spilled. Luc wasn't up for it. Let him and his pal Claire get into a screaming fight here, in front of the tourists.

The waiter brought him another scotch without being asked. All right, one more drink. They didn't have any at home, after all. "I can't believe you buy into all that crap, Claire. They're just twins. They're innocent. Neither one has much power. Don't worry about it."

"They have power," Richard said in a low voice. He looked up at Luc, his eyes unreadable. "They have power over you, over . . . all of us."

Luc shook his head impatiently. "Fairy tales. The *famille* probably made it all up to keep kids in line."

Both Richard and Claire looked at him solemnly, identical glassy-eyed gazes not hiding their sharp intelligence, their experience. All of it hard-won.

He shook his head again and took a gulp of his drink. "You worry too much."

"Uh-*huh*," I said, not crossing the threshold.

Kevin looked at me innocently. "What?"

"No one else is home, and we're going to go in and watch a movie. I'm using air quotes around 'watch a movie.'"

He laughed and took my hand, gently pulling me through the back door of his enormous house. Inside it was dark and cool. A clock chimed somewhere—it was eight thirty.

"Who checked on the movie times?" he asked.

"Me," I admitted. The web site had been wrong, and we'd missed the first twenty minutes of what we'd wanted to see. Kevin had said we could watch a movie at his house. But I had expected at least one of his parents to be home.

"Don't you want to see *Before the Day?*"

"Yes, but—" The house stretched out all around us, pristine and decorated and bigger than any private house I'd ever been in. I loved the fourteen-foot ceilings, the tall French windows, the gleaming wide floorboards.

Kevin quit tugging on my hand. "Hey, if you don't want to stay—that's cool. We can go somewhere else, do something else. I wasn't trying to push you."

That was one reason why I liked Kevin so much. He was totally sincere about that. I mean, Luc might have said the same thing, but he wouldn't have meant it as much, would really wanted me to change my mind. Kevin was willing to take me at face value.

Don't think about Luc.

"I'm assuming the TV is downstairs?"

Kevin grinned. "I was thinking the one up in my room."

Laughing, I pushed against his chest gently. "Think again."

He raised his hands in defeat and led me into a family room that was bigger than the front room and workroom at Petra's house put together. He opened an antique-looking entertainment center to reveal a gigantic TV.

"Oh my God," I said enviously, and he smiled.

"You'll have to come to our Super Bowl party. Or maybe not—it gets pretty ugly. You want something to drink? I can make popcorn."

I just gazed at him in appreciation. He would have been so perfect—if I didn't have the memory of someone else.

"Is this okay?" Kevin's voice was muffled and kind of hoarse.

Feeling like I was about to jump off a cliff, I managed to nod before our mouths met again. The only light was a dim table lamp across the room. We were lying on the wide sectional sofa, making out, the movie a muted background noise that we hadn't paid any attention to. Kevin was a great kisser, smooth and sure and gentle, with an underlying determination. It was . . . really nice. Great, even. But my brain never went haywire, I never lost myself, never felt like we were becoming one person. I really, really liked holding him, liked the way he felt and kissed, felt comfortable making out but didn't feel desperate to go further. I didn't feel like being more assertive or demanding as much as I was giving.

We were lying side by side, and now he put his hand on my leg, right below where my dress ended. His hand slid up my thigh slowly, giving me time to stop him.

"Um," I said, breaking away from our kiss. I felt sleepy and dopey and thoroughly kissed, and it was so nice, such a good feeling. Breathing hard, Kevin waited, then leaned in and kissed my neck, sending shivers down my spine. His hand went a little higher, and it was exciting—it felt risky and safe at the same time, and part of me wanted to see where it would lead.

Except I knew where it would lead, and I couldn't go there.

I put my hand over his, and he stopped, pulling back to look at me.

"I want to touch you," he whispered, kissing the

side of my face. He felt warm and so, so nice, and it was incredibly tempting. If I could have said yes, I would have.

But I couldn't.

"I . . . can't," I whispered back. I remembered how angry Chad Woolcott had been, the ugly fight we'd had, where his nice facade had dropped away, leaving a hateful jackass. *Please don't let that happen now.*

Kevin hesitated, and I imagined the war inside his head—push now and see if she gives in, be a good guy now and see if it pays off later. . . .

He took his hand away. Holding me in an embrace, he kissed my face and then my mouth, snuggling closer.

I couldn't relax. "Are you . . . okay?"

He looked at me and gave a little smile. "I'm here with you. Everything's fine."

I relaxed and right then became aware of a dull humming sound. "What's that? Is that . . . just the fridge or something?"

Kevin listened, then he sat up and tugged his shirt down. "Oops. That's the driveway gate opening. Someone's home." His smile was beautiful and teasing as I bolted into a sitting position and smoothed out my clothes.

Getting up with quick grace, Kevin flicked on several more lamps. I grabbed the remote and turned up the TV's volume. And there we were, watching a movie neither of us could name, when Kevin's stepmother came in.

"Kev?" a woman called.

"Hey," Kevin called back, Mr. Innocent. I gave him a look and he smirked at me.

After a moment she came into the family room, sorting through a thick stack of mail. "Hi, sweetie," she said without looking up. "I saw your car. Didn't you have a date tonight?"

She was tall and elegant, with black hair swept up into a chignon. Even Clio would have approved of her tailored—probably designer—pantsuit.

"Uh, yeah," Kevin said, muting the TV again. "This is Thais. Thais, this is my mom."

His stepmother looked up sharply and saw me. I projected an air of goody two-shoes while her eyes narrowed at Kevin.

"Nice to meet you, Mrs. LaTour," I said politely.

"You too, sweetie," she said to me, then turned her attention to Kevin. "Home alone with a girl? Minus five points."

He looked a little embarrassed while she made a big show of examining the situation. My cheeks started to heat up.

"But you're downstairs. Plus two points. And everyone's clothes are on. Another two points."

Now I was mortified.

"So it could be worse," she said, putting the mail down on a bookshelf. "I'm not trying to embarrass you, sweetie." Her eyes were kind as she looked at me. "But Kevin's father and I know how easy it is to get carried away, make a mistake."

"Mom," Kevin groaned, putting his head in his hands.

"Especially in a house with a liquor cabinet and a swimming pool."

"The liquor cabinet's locked!" Kevin protested.

"I don't drink," I said quickly.

"We're almost eighteen," Kevin pointed out.

"Yes, and eighteen is a great age to get married and have babies," Mrs. LaTour said brightly. "Or better yet, to have babies and *not* get married. I mean, college, schmollege! Careers are for losers! Right?"

Kevin just groaned, shaking his head in his hands.

I wished I could melt into the couch and disappear. How would I ever be able to face his stepmom again?

"We were just watching a movie," I said faintly, my face burning. I could never come back to this house, never meet Kevin's dad—not after tonight. She'd tell him that Kevin had been making out with some girl, and that would have been me, and I would never—

Believe me.

The thought flew away from me as if it had its own destination.

Believe what you see, not what you fear.

Have trust in your child whose heart you hold dear.

I hadn't meant to send it out, wasn't even sure what it would do. But I was so embarrassed and mortified and just wanted this to end.

Mrs. LaTour blinked and put her head to one side, and then she leaned against the doorway into the kitchen. "Gosh, I'm . . . so tired," she said, sounding sapped. "I didn't realize it." She looked up at us. "What was I saying?"

"Um," Kevin said.

"Well, it's late—I really should get going," I said. "I have a curfew." I didn't really, but let her think of me as the nice girl with the curfew.

"All right . . . Thais, is it?"

I nodded.

"I'll take you," Kevin said, practically springing off the couch.

"It was nice to meet you, Mrs. LaTour," I said.

"Dr.," Kevin whispered. "Dr. Hendricks."

"Sorry. Dr. Hendricks," I said. I grabbed the sweater Clio hadn't wanted me to bring, and Kevin and I hightailed it out of there.

When he dropped me off at home, Clio's car was still gone. Kevin walked me up to the porch, and we stood out of the streetlight's glare for a while, kissing and murmuring goodbyes.

"I'm sorry my mom walked in on us," he said.

"It's okay," I said. "But I was so embarrassed."

"She'll forget about it," he promised.

Yeah, I think she will. I found that unsettling.

Finally we tore ourselves away from each other and I went inside. Dropping my purse on the little table by the front door, I headed back to find Petra. Sure enough, the kitchen lights were on. I felt Clio in the house, which was weird . . .

Except, when I reached the kitchen, she was sitting there with Petra at the table. They both looked grim. *Uh-oh*, I thought. *What now?*

"I didn't see your car," I said. "I thought you were still out."

"There's a reason for that," Clio said bitterly.

"I've been trying to call you," Petra said.

Frowning, I pulled my cell out of my purse. I hadn't turned it on. "Oh."

Then they told me about how, while I'd been making out with my boyfriend, my twin sister had almost been killed. Again.

My first thought was: *Melita?*

Get Over Her

The French Quarter had sunk even lower into its iniquity. It had been forty years since Marcel had been here. It had been shocking then, but now it was like he was at the entrance to hell.

Well, he'd seen enough. Here, surrounded by gaudy lights, gaudy people, horrid scents, and ear-deafening noise, he missed his home at the monastery with a raw pain. He would never be able to go back. Something would happen here to prevent it; he was sure of it. How could he return to Father Jonah with fresh blood on his hands?

He turned and headed back up to St. Charles Avenue. It was three in the morning—it might take a while for the streetcar to come. Not many locals would wait for it at this hour—crime had spiraled so far out of control that most natives lived behind locked iron gates, burglar alarms, and private security firms.

However, Marcel didn't worry about getting mugged. He had nothing to lose, not even his life.

As he walked past a place Ouida had taken him

to for lunch back in the fifties, the door swung open and three drunks stumbled out, laughing and holding on to each other for support. They almost ran right into him and he stepped back, weary and revolted.

Oh.

He knew these drunks. They were three of his least-favorite people in the whole world.

They were gasping with laughter and righted themselves clumsily.

"Oh, pardon me," said Claire, blinking hazily up at him. Then her face changed with recognition and she stood up straighter. "Marcel."

Richard and Luc also straightened, as if they were willing themselves to sober up to deal with him. Maybe they were—frivolously doing system-cleaning spells to rid themselves of pollutants. It would be just like them to misuse magickal power. He himself hadn't used or made magick in a long, long time—not since he'd devoted his life to the Christian God, back in 1919. He tried not to even think about magick. It wasn't up to mere humans to bend the power of God to their will, and that was what magick was. Only the hand of God should alter things out of their natural paths.

Looking at these three, he knew that distinction was lost on them. He tried to keep his face impassive but felt his lip curl slightly in disgust. Of course Luc was still completely dissolute. Where were this week's women? Usually he had two or three hanging off him.

And Richard.

Richard was the embodiment of the hand of God, put on earth to humble Marcel and remind him of his all-too-human weaknesses. To hate someone as deeply as he hated Richard, to be stirred to violence at just the sight of him—these were tragic character flaws that Marcel had spent decades trying to improve.

Without success.

"Marcel," said Luc. He held out a hand. "Sorry you got brought back like that. Daedalus is having another lust-for-power banquet. You and Claire were the appetizer."

Marcel forced himself to shake Luc's hand.

"Luc."

"I got in Thursday," Claire said. She fished a crumpled pack of cigarettes out of her big, lumpy purse and lit one.

"Tobacco," Marcel said. "Satan's agent. Slavery, cancer, corporate lies, deliberate poison—it all stems from the tobacco industry."

"Glad you've lightened up," Luc muttered.

Claire looked at Marcel and blew smoke away from them, out the side of her mouth. "Marcel, honey, you must have missed the memo. There is no Satan. No Satan, no hell. We've got *la déesse, le dieu,* the life force that exists in everything. We've got ourselves and our free will. You can't pretend to believe different."

"I don't believe different," Marcel said. "I *know* different. There's the one true God, his Holy Son,

144

the Holy Spirit. And there is surely Satan and surely hell." He'd seen both, close up.

Claire let out a deep breath. "Okay. Tomato, tomah-to. Anyway, we've been talking about possible ways to kill Daedalus." Her face brightened, and Luc smiled again. "Got any ideas?"

"If I had, I would have used them long ago, before I committed my soul to God. But not necessarily on Daedalus."

From the corner of his eye, he saw Richard's muscles tense. Looking at him straight on, Marcel saw a mirror of his own hatred and resentment.

Luc sighed and rolled his eyes.

"Damn it!" Claire smacked him on the chest with her fist, surprising him. She looked back and forth between him and Richard furiously. "Damn both of you! That was two hundred and fifty years ago! Get *over* it! Ger over *her*! You stupid jackasses! Just let it *go*!" Some people walking by stopped to watch the spectacle unfolding.

Richard and Luc looked as surprised as Marcel felt. Claire had always been a drama queen, but she'd never spoken to them like this before. Pain and heartache bored her, she'd said. She'd rather just have fun.

She spoke again, her voice low and trembling with anger. "You're both so *stupid*, so *blind*. Centuries later and she's still squeezing your hearts. Cerise was a sweet girl—she didn't deserve what happened to her. Goddess knows we've been playing out the tragedy ever since. But you two are the most single-minded idiots I've ever—you're *pathetic*, both of you. Poor Marcel. Poor Richard. Lost their true love."

Marcel stepped back, stung, feeling blood burn his cheeks.

"All this time, it's always been Cerise, Cerise, Cerise," Claire went on. She seemed stone-cold sober now, her green eyes fiery. "You can't even *see* anyone else. You can't even *recognize* love—" She stopped abruptly, shutting her mouth like a trap. White-faced with anger, she glared at them for a second more, then rubbed her hand over her eyes. "I'm tired," she said. "I'm going back to Jules's."

Without another word she turned and crossed the street, heading away from the lights on Chartres Street. She seemed to be weaving a bit, and after a pause Luc said, "I'll go with her, make sure she gets back."

Then he was gone, leaving Marcel and Richard facing each other. Marcel's head was spinning. What had Claire meant?

Richard was watching him steadily, but Marcel knew he was just as shaken.

"She's talking rot," he heard himself say. "She's drunk. As usual. Doesn't know what she's talking about."

Richard, barely two feet away, close enough to strangle, gave him an odd smile. "Claire always knows what she's talking about. She knows more than you and me put together. Despite everything you learned, being Melita's bitch half your life."

Pain stabbed Marcel's heart so strongly he

almost gasped. He actually staggered, one hand on his chest, and leaned against the crumbling stucco of the Napoleon House. Several people glanced at him in alarm, but they faded away, out of his sight. All he could see was Richard's face, that hateful, beautiful angel's face that Cerise hadn't been able to resist.

"How did you—" he choked. "Who else knows? How could you—"

But Richard only gave him another small, tight smile, then turned and walked away.

Clio

Another sleepless night. I was exhausted to my bones—this day had been endless and the evening horrible. Every time I closed my eyes, I saw my Camry billowing black smoke toward the sky.

Okay, okay, Clio, think. Think it all through. Someone is trying to kill you or Thais—again. The more I thought about Thais's theory about Melita, the less ridiculous it seemed. Sure, it was a stretch, but none of this made sense anyway. The only reason I could think of for anyone wanting me or Thais out of the way was if the *two* of us made more than a full Treize. Daedalus needed a full Treize—but no more—for the rite. Someone needed one of us gone before the rite. As much as I was drawn to working with Hermann Parfitte's book, as much as I needed to know how to control the rite's power, still, I needed to know who was behind the attacks more.

If we knew that, then other things would fall into place.

At least, I hoped so.

Okay. Now I knew what I needed to do. I got out of bed and walked quietly into Thais's room. She was deeply asleep, her layered black hair in an aureole around her head. Kneeling next to the bed, I shook her shoulder.

"Thais," I said softly. "Thais, wake up."

She stirred, then blinked. Her eyes focused on me and she instantly looked alarmed. "What is it? Are you okay?" Sitting up, she looked at me anxiously.

"Hi," I whispered. "Sorry to wake you. But I need you for something."

"What?" She rubbed her eyes, still looking worried. "What's wrong?"

"I'll explain on the way," I said. "First we have to steal Nan's car."

No one did stiff disapproval better than Thais. I had to hand it to her. She was much better than Nan, even.

Now she sat next to me in the front seat of Nan's Volvo. The only time she'd uncrossed her arms had been to eat a McBiscuit.

"Since I'm going to get hanged when we go back, can you fill me in on what my crime is going to be?"

"Yeah. Right now we're going to a safe place so we can do a spell," I explained. "Last night—was it only last night? God. Last night someone blew up my car. There's so much going on so, so much crazy stuff, but if someone out there *is* still trying

149

to hurt us, the most important thing is finding out who it is. When we know that, we can figure out how to protect ourselves from them and figure out how it relates to the rite. We can't even plan what to do in the rite until we know who's behind the attacks."

I glanced at her, making a mental note to avoid ever pulling that face.

Thais let out a heavy breath and looked out her window. "The rite."

"Yes."

"Where you want us to become immortal."

"Yes. Thais, I've thought and thought about it. We can't die. We have to go on living like this, young and beautiful and healthy. Think of everything we could do with all that time to do it in."

"Yeah, and it's worked out so well for the Treize," she said sarcastically. "They're the poster children for mental health and stability."

"We're different. We're choosing this on purpose. We have goals for ourselves, our lives. They weren't prepared."

"I'm not prepared either."

I stayed quiet, letting her wrap her mind around the idea. Several miles later, she finally spoke.

"I've thought about it. I just don't know. I think the rite is going to kill someone, like it killed Cerise."

"Not if we know who to protect ourselves from,"

I pointed out. "Not if we're strong. Not if we're the ones controlling it."

She shook her head, looking out her window. Her face was troubled, reluctant. "We're just going to set something on fire again," she said.

"Not if we're in the middle of a river."

"They don't make floating cups?" Thais asked.

"No. But we can do this without the four element cups," I said. We were waist-deep in a small river close to the town of Abita Springs. The water was red and cold, mostly clear. Where we were, the river was about forty feet wide. I wished Racey were with us—remembering what had happened the other times that Thais and I had made magick together didn't reassure me. But Nan hadn't been able to figure out who was trying to hurt us, and now my frigging *car* had been blown up. I just had to do something.

"Maybe we should talk about this some more," Thais said, eyeing my supplies.

"Look, we have to do this," I said. "Once we know who's trying to kill us, we'll be able to focus on the rite and on becoming immortal." I realized how bizarre my words were, and how they actually made sense in the craziness of our lives, and laughed.

"You must have been a fun child," said Thais.

I laughed again, glad that we were together, that it was daylight, that we were far away from anyone.

"Okay, we're standing in water, which is your

element," I said. "So this should be good." Glancing at the sky, I saw that it was still clouded over. It didn't look like rain was near, though. The only candle I'd been able to find that would float was a goofy one in the shape of a yellow duck. I lit it, and then I dropped four stones in the water around us: one for the past, one for the future, one for now, and one for the problem. Thais and I held hands over the water, and I began to recite:

> We walk in sunlight
> Shadows follow us.
> We are facing fire
> We are standing beneath stone
> We are underwater
> A storm is coming toward us.
> With these words reveal the signature
> Give the shadow a face, a name
> Show us who kindles fire against us
> Who holds a stone over us
> Who pulls us underwater
> Who conjures a storm to destroy us.

I began my song. The last time I'd done a spell, I'd taken Q-Tip's soul from him. That had been a huge and powerful spell, and this was another one. Beneath my nervousness and determination, I felt deeply tired and tainted. *Maybe Melita began like this.* I don't know where the thought came from, but it chilled me. I pushed it down and kept singing, closing my eyes, trying to concentrate.

Thais didn't join in, but I felt her power rising with mine, joining mine through our clasped hands. And I really did actually *feel* her power—it had become tangible, stronger, since the last time we'd done a spell together.

Ideally, a photographic image would have popped up in our minds, with a big yellow arrow pointing to the guilty party. But nooo. Magick doesn't work like that. You have to meet it halfway.

I sang for a while; I don't know how long. I was getting nothing and decided this was a bust. I quit singing and opened my eyes to tell Thais. She opened her eyes at the exact same time, and we stood looking at each other for a moment. In the next second, I was pulled into her eyes, the green striations like veins on a leaf. It was like sinking into a vortex, like a wormhole in a sci-fi movie. In the depths of her eyes, I started getting images.

There was the hazy outline of my car, like a smudged Polaroid. I saw a dark figure off to the distance, and somehow I knew its lips were moving, its hands making motions, but I couldn't tell if it was a man or a woman.

I saw my car explode into flames again, and I winced. Like in a fuzzy old movie, I saw myself, a blurred stick figure, jump out of the car and run away, and I felt someone's dark pangs of disappointment that I hadn't died.

It made my blood boil.

More images flowed. I saw Thais sitting on a

streetcar, saw a red pickup fly soundlessly through the air, snapping a light pole in slow motion. Inside the streetcar, Thais got to her feet and moved out of the pole's way, seconds before it would have impaled her.

Was Thais seeing this? I blinked several times, trying to retreat to see her, but I couldn't—my spell had unlocked this knowledge, and it had to spool out until it was finished.

I was sleeping in bed—no, it was Thais sleeping. Her sheet twisted thickly and coiled around her neck. She began choking, flailing, trying to pull it off. It must have been so terrifying. . . . Next, Thais and I were standing in front of our house, under the streetlight. A huge dark cloud engulfed us, and I grimaced, remembering the searing pain of the thousands of wasp stings that had almost killed us.

Next I got to relive that scuzzy guy pulling a knife on me in the alley in the Quarter. I felt the fear all over again, the cold pounding of my heart, my numb lips as I tried to summon a spell. Luc had run up right afterward.

Had it been Luc all along?

The images got smaller, farther away, and I thought, *No*, because I hadn't learned anything. Again I saw the same things happening—the streetcar, the wasps, the mugging—but now I saw another person at the edge of each scene, someone standing, watching, working the spells that called the danger to us. Who was it? *Reveal yourself!*

The figure sharpened, took on features, clothing . . . and I felt like I had been clubbed on the head with a brick. It was *Richard. Richard* watching the streetcar and feeling disappointed that Thais hadn't died. *Richard* summoning the wasps, watching them surround us, *Richard* working the spell to choke Thais with her sheet, *Richard* compelling that poor sap to attack me.

I couldn't breathe, couldn't get air. In my mind I saw Richard and me tumbling on his bed, me pushing his shirt off, holding him tightly, holding his head and kissing him, wanting him, *burning* for him. He had tried to kill me and Thais, again and again.

Oh God, I was going to be sick.

With a heaving gulp I fell backward, breaking the spell. I splashed down into the water. It closed over my head, but I forced my legs to straighten and righted myself, gagging and holding my stomach.

Thais grabbed my arm. "Are you okay?" She sounded near tears. "Did you see Richard?"

I was barely able to nod, trying to control the dry heaves that shook me.

"I can't believe it," Thais said. "I just can't believe it!"

"It's true," I choked. And then I felt a huge, dark presence well up behind me. A shadow fell on Thais's face, and she looked up. Her eyes widened and her mouth opened.

Turning, I saw we'd created a waterspout, a tornado made of river water, and it was spinning at us with a hissing howl, faster than I'd ever seen something move.

In one second the twenty-foot cyclone of water swallowed us, gulping us greedily into its unnatural strength. I tried to hold on to Thais, to scream, to summon a spell to save us—but our hands were wrenched apart. The last thing I saw was Thais's pale, terrified face whirling away from me in the side of the cyclone.

The Bottom

Something was wrong.

Petra awoke in an instant, as she always did. Unconsciously she cast her senses throughout the house and yard, taking a quick reading of her world.

The twins weren't here. She couldn't detect their vibrations anywhere in the house or yard.

A glance at her clock showed six forty-five. On a Sunday, she could count on Clio sleeping in till ten. Leaping up, Petra began muttering reveal spells that would reveal whether someone had lured the twins away magickally. Two minutes later she knew that they had left of their own accord, not too long before, and that they had taken *her car*. And would be grounded until they were in their late twenties.

She grabbed the phone as she pulled on some baggy gardener's pants. "Ouida? I need your help."

"This way?" Melysa looked to the right.

Ouida nodded, her eyes vacant. She and Petra sat in the backseat, holding hands. Together their concentration was revealing the twins' route, all the way to Abita Springs. Abita Springs! What were they up to? Petra's mouth set in a grim line. She knew it wasn't good. They weren't over here at a pick-your-own pumpkin patch.

Melysa turned to the right and headed down a narrow, barely paved road.

"A river," Petra murmured, seeing it in her mind. Then she and Ouida sat up straight at the same time.

"Oh goddess," Ouida breathed.

She heard it before she saw it. As she, Ouida, and Melysa crashed through the woods toward the river, Petra heard a high wailing sound, like a train engine. The closer they got to the river, the more leaves and twigs whipped through the air. They tangled in Melysa's hair and scratched Petra's face.

"Is it a tornado?" Melysa called over the rising sound.

Then they saw it: a muddy waterspout spinning its way across the river toward the shore. Its sides were blotched with dark objects, pieces of driftwood, a snake, some fish. And the merest glimpse of a pale face, pale arms pinned within the wall of water.

Instantly the three witches flung their arms out and began shouting a dissipation spell. Each one used a version unique to herself, but the forms were the same, and they all had the same goal. Petra felt every muscle in her body quiver with magick as she called on a deeper power than she had used in decades.

"Water, lie down in your bed!" she commanded,

holding out her wand. Electricity crackled around her, though she couldn't see it. Behind her Ouida and Melysa were chanting and drawing sigils in the air. "Water, lie down in your bed!" Petra shouted, feeling as if her magick were going to sweep her up into its arms and fling her into the air.

Then it stopped. The waterspout fell all at once, smashing down into the river. Two human figures lay crumpled in shallow water, twenty yards away. Petra raced toward them, already calling on healing powers.

She reached Thais first and dragged her up onto land. The girl was unconscious but breathing. Ouida ran up and took over while Petra splashed into the river to get Clio. Clio's eyes fluttered and she raised her head weakly, but she collapsed again and would have gone under if Petra hadn't grabbed her arms. Melysa supported Clio's other side, and together they dragged her onto the small sandy shore. In addition to the spells they were muttering, they pounded the girls firmly on their backs. At last the twins started coughing and gagging up water.

"They look like drowned rats," Melysa muttered, wiping Thais's hair away from her face.

Clio's eyes opened blearily and she looked around, trying to orient herself.

Petra held Clio's head in her lap, stroking her hair. "Clio, are you all right?"

Clio blinked several times, finally placing where she was and what had happened. "Thais?" she said hoarsely.

"Will be fine," said Ouida, kneeling in the sand next to her. "*What* were you two *doing?*"

"I'm sorry, Nan," Clio croaked, struggling to sit up. Petra helped her, supporting her back. Her anger had been tempered by the girls' danger and her relief at their safety.

"I'm sorry. But we had to know who was trying to hurt us. I had to know who blew up my *car*." Clio's eyes were brighter and her voice stronger. Petra recognized Clio's sense of outrage and knew that it wasn't in her personality to take anything lying down.

"You almost got yourselves killed!" Petra said. "Did you cause this, or was this another attack?"

"Flip a coin," Thais said weakly, also sitting up. Her face was still pale, and she had an ugly bruise already developing on one shoulder.

"I'm not sure," said Clio, looking thoughtful. "I thought we had done it, putting our magick together. But I guess it's possible. . . ." Suddenly her eyes flared and her face looked furious. "It was Richard, Nan!" She grabbed Petra's arm and shook it. "It was Richard! Richard who's been trying to kill us! We saw it!"

"*What?*" Petra was shocked. Of all the people she'd suspected, none of them had been Richard.

Thais nodded, getting stiffly to her feet. She had sand in her hair and dripping off her clothes. "It's true, if that spell worked. We saw him casting the spells, waiting to see what happened. *Richard.*" She sounded angry and sad, but Clio had sounded truly incensed, as if she were taking the news more personally.

Petra met Ouida's eyes. Ouida looked as shocked as Petra felt.

"*Richard,*" Ouida repeated, amazed.

Grimly, Petra got to her feet and helped Clio stand. "I'm surprised, but I can't say it's completely unthinkable. But this ends *now.* Melysa, can you drive the girls back home? And stay with them till I get back? Do not let them out of your sight, okay?"

Melysa nodded solemnly. "Yes. Ouida, are you coming with me or going with Petra?"

"I need to see Richard alone, I think," Petra said, brushing sand off her wet canvas pants.

"I'm sure we'll be okay," Clio began. "We don't need a babysitter. We'll be fine—"

Petra gave her a piercing glare. "You will stay *home,* with Melysa, until I get back. You will not leave the house, not even to take the *garbage* out. You will not be taking anyone's *car* without permission, you will not *leave* Melysa's side, or I will slap you with a homing spell so strong you'll live out the rest of your life in your *rooms.* Understand?"

A mulish look crossed Clio's face as she weighed Petra's words. She must have realized that Petra was dead serious, because she shrugged ungraciously and said, "Whatever."

The five of them started to trudge back to their cars. Petra couldn't believe she'd almost lost the girls today. In their headstrong *stupidity.* She walked

161

closer to Clio and put her arm around the girl's shoulders. "I don't want you hurt."

"I know."

"I can't believe it's Richard. But I'll get to the bottom of this, I promise."

Clio looked up at her and gave a tiny smile. "Okay."

"I just can't imagine—" Petra thought out loud. "I wonder . . . does it have something to do with you two looking like Cerise?"

Next to her, Clio stopped in her tracks. "We look like Cerise?"

"Yes, of course. Didn't you see her in your visions?"

"I told you that," Thais said. "We look just like Cerise; we did see it in our vision."

Clio shook her head slowly. "Not clearly enough to see her face. It was dark and rainy."

"I saw her," Thais said. "And we do look like her, except she was blond."

Petra saw the two girls exchange a look.

"I'm sorry," she told Clio, continuing on to her car. "I thought you knew that." As always, her heart felt pained at the memory of the night she'd lost her last two remaining children.

"How much alike?" Clio asked.

"Exactly," Petra said sadly, opening her car door. "You two look exactly like Cerise, but with black hair. But other than that, spitting image."

Ouida nodded, looking sympathetic. "She was a beautiful girl, as you two are."

Petra watched her girls get bundled into Melysa's car. Melysa had thought to bring large beach towels, and now she made sure the twins were wrapped up warmly. Petra followed Melysa's car all the way back to New Orleans, until Melysa took the Carrollton exit off the highway, and Petra continued on to the French Quarter.

When They Had Met

Each day was a blessing. Each day when he opened his eyes, whether it was sunny, rainy, clammy, or freezing, he was glad to be alive. It hadn't always been that way.

Jules got up out of his single bed and stretched. It was raining lightly—he heard it pattering against the roof. The floor beneath his feet was cool—could autumn really be showing her face? He moved quietly, like a cat, into the bathroom, glancing into the front room as he did. Claire was asleep on the couch, in her clothes. He'd heard her come in early this morning, heard Luc put her to bed. She hadn't changed her ways. She never would.

It was strange, really, how little any of them had changed over such a long period of time. Not only had they been frozen in age, but in their personalities too. You'd think that over almost two hundred and fifty years, at least some of them would have undergone huge changes, but none of them ever really had. Certainly not him.

Back in the kitchen he put the kettle on to make coffee. Claire would want some when she woke up.

The small window over his kitchen sink had an uninspiring view of the brick fence next door, covered with fig ivy. In the front room, Claire stirred, shifting position, curling up almost like a child on the narrow futon couch. She'd teased him about his meager surroundings. Told him he still thought like a slave, after centuries of freedom. He admitted it was true. Slavery was not something one ever really got over.

In the kettle, the water made a rough purring sound. It was about to boil. He got out the sugar cubes, knowing Claire usually took three.

In some ways, it seemed just a short while ago that he had met her.

He'd run away from the tobacco farmer who owned him. He'd been beaten badly, and his hands had been manacled, but he'd escaped. He'd wandered for days, moving as he could, though in the end it was more like crawling. He reached a swamp and was only five feet into it when he fell, tripping on a hidden root, splashing down, hitting his head on another root. The world swirled, and he smiled, because now he was dying. They hadn't found him, and now they would find only a corpse. He almost laughed, thinking how furious they would be. The top of his head, his face, was barely out of the water. It was warm and pleasant. Surely it wouldn't take long now.

But . . . being dead couldn't hurt this much, could it? He was in so much pain it shocked him. The bumping, the jolting . . . He forced himself to open his eyes. *Please let me be dead. Please, please let me see nothing, see the white men's angels, see devils, see anything but—*

Trees. Above him were trees. It was barely light out, but whether it was dawn or twilight, he couldn't tell. He was being dragged somewhere. He was alive. Tears escaped his eyes and rolled down the drying mud on his face. A rolling boom of thunder made him tremble, and then warm rain was pelting him through the trees.

A face looked back at him. A white face, with orange hair and blue eyes. A boy. The boy was dragging him on a plank over the ground. The boy would take him back to the farm, turn him in, collect his ten dollars.

Crying, he'd raised his hands to his face, but the manacles were heavy and he banged himself on the nose. The white boy looked back at him, then rested the plank on the ground and came to kneel by his head. He tried to stop crying, tried to look brave, like a man, but he wasn't a man—he had no name.

The white boy spoke in French. *"Vous serez récuperer, m'sieu,"* he said in a soft voice. *"À mon ville, pas loin. Calmez-vous."*

Those words made no sense.

That had been Marcel who'd found him in the swamp, dying, and fashioned a travois out of a plank and dragged him three miles to Ville du Bois. Twelve-year-old Marcel turned him over to Petra, the healer. Jules burned with fever for a week, hallucinating, rigid with terror. Petra made him teas and soups, some bitter, some not. She washed the swamp mud off him, put salve on all his injuries. The smith came and broke the manacles off his hands.

"*Vous vous appelle Jules,*" Petra murmured one night, late, just after his fever had broken. "*Vous vous serez appeller Jules maintenant.*"

A dark-haired man came in. Armand. He explained things to Jules in English. And when Jules recovered, as Marcel had said he would, he stayed there, in the Ville du Bois, living as one of them, as a person, for the first time in his life. It was a hidden paradise. Jules never ventured far from the village— misery and pain waited outside. He never wanted to leave—everyone was so kind. M. Daedalus taught him to read and write. Everyone, even the children, helped teach him the natural religion, the *bonne magie.* It fell into place in his life, like tumblers in a lock being set into place with the right key.

One day, some ten years after he'd arrived, he talked to Claire for the first time. He knew what the village said about her—that she had loose skirts— but it wasn't like back in the other world, where she would have been beaten or exiled.

Jules had been walking home, a string of catfish over his shoulder. As he walked, he murmured a litany of thanks for everything he had, everything he saw around him, every scrap of happiness he felt. He gave thanks for all of it as often as he could.

Not far from the village, he heard voices raised in anger. Several more steps showed him Claire and a young man—Etienne somebody—arguing.

Claire slapped Etienne with her free hand. Fury washed Etienne's face with an ugly red hue, and he raised his fist above Claire's head. Just as he was sweeping it down, Jules grabbed it from behind.

"Now, now," Jules said, keeping his own anger firmly locked away, "you know we don't hit women."

"Mind your own business, old man!" Etienne snapped.

"This *is* my business," Jules said. His strong fingers pried Etienne's hand off Claire's arm, and she fell to the ground, then scrambled to her feet. "I'm stopping you from making a mistake that will haunt your soul. You know the threefold law."

Etienne sneered. "That's only for magick, old fool!"

"No," Jules replied, shaking his head. "It's for everything, all the time."

"You'd best let me go," Etienne snarled, "and continue on your way. This is between me and my girl."

"I'm not your girl!" Claire said.

"You're everybody's girl." The disdain on Etienne's face pained Jules. The younger man turned back to him. "Last warning. You let me go now, or—" He showed Jules his clenched fist.

"I'm not a girl you can threaten, boy," Jules said mildly. "And my fist is bigger than yours."

It was almost twice as big, in fact: Jules was a much bigger man than most of the villagers—the little French people, as he thought of them.

Etienne looked at Jules's huge fist, with its fingers that had been broken and not set properly. He

168

looked at Jules's face, which was not mean but iron hard. Jules saw the moment when the boy realized that Jules was maybe seven inches taller and had about fifty pounds on him.

The fight faded from the younger man. The fight, but not the fury.

"Have it your way," he spat, and wrenched his hand loose.

"I'll be upset if I hear you've bothered this young lady again," Jules said.

"She's no lady," Etienne tossed over his shoulder.

It deserved no response.

"Are you all right?"

Claire nodded. "Thank you." She seemed embarrassed and unsure of herself, very different from the brash, flirtatious girl Jules saw around the village.

They began walking together.

"It's a shame our paradise is marred by one like him," Jules said.

"Paradise!" Claire stared at him. "You mean prison! I would give anything to leave! In fact, Etienne had promised to take me to New Orleans if I lay with him. But he was lying."

"This village is the last Eden on earth," Jules said seriously. "The world out there is full of pain."

He saw her glancing at his scars from back on the farm.

"I'm smothering here, day by day," Claire said. "I've got to get out." She stopped in the path and looked at him, her eyes clear and without guile. "If you ever leave here, take me with you."

He almost lost his breath. What was she saying?

Oh. That she wanted someone to protect her on the way or a mule or horse to ride, if he had one.

"I won't be leaving, *mamzelle*," he said gruffly. "You take care now." He split off from the path and followed another to his own little house, his sanctuary.

"Hey."

Jules jumped as Claire shuffled up and reached for a coffee cup. It was now again, and the memories of then twisted away like leaves in a breeze.

"Time is it?" she mumbled, pouring coffee.

"Not quite noon."

Her magenta hair smelled like cigarette smoke. She had four small silver rings in her left ear. Jules was thankful she'd let her brow piercing heal over.

"How was it last night?" Jules asked.

Claire shrugged, leaning against the kitchen counter. "All right. Ran into Marcel."

"Then Daedalus will want to convene the Treize soon, now that you two are here."

Claire's face looked bleak as she sipped her coffee. "Yep."

Clio

I lay on my bed, my wet hair making my T-shirt soggy. Thais and I had both had hot showers, and Melysa and Ouida had made us valerian-and-catnip tea. Now I lay on my bed, feeling Melysa and Thais's presence downstairs.

Richard was the one who'd been trying to kill us. Richard, who I'd jumped just two days ago and practically slept with. *How could he?* He had actually tried to *kill* me. *And* sleep with me. He was a total *psychopath*. It was terrifying—especially since I hadn't seen it in him, hadn't felt it. Hadn't seen it in his eyes or felt it in his touch. What was wrong with me that I hadn't picked up on it? The same thing with Luc—they had been both pursuing me and simultaneously betraying me. The two of them.

What was wrong with me? Here's what was worse: knowing Richard had tried to kill us made me feel pretty murderous myself. And goddess knew Luc was still on my "forget it" list. *Yet*—I still wondered what was wrong with me that they didn't just love me. Which was so twisted and pathetic and unhealthy that I started bawling all over again, pressing my face into my pillow so no one would hear.

Luc had wanted me because I was the missing part of Thais. Petra wondered if Richard trying to kill us had anything to do with our looking like Cerise, whom he had loved. Did he only see me as a modern version of Cerise?

I almost cried myself sick, working through half a box of tissues, crying until my guts felt twisted and raw. How many times was I going to cry over guys? It had already been too many.

Another question: when could I escape to go confront Richard myself? Because I was going to rip his lungs out. Somehow I didn't feel afraid of him now, or worried about what he might do next. It was like knowing who it was had granted me immunity from his attacks. I was burning with fury, itching to take it out on him. As soon as I got a chance.

Someone Unseen

Daedalus opened his eyes slowly. The sky had clouded over significantly in the hour since he'd started his spell. The sounds of the swamp were intensifying as twilight neared—animals were foraging, birds going on the hunt—he was making magick. The palm of his right hand tingled, and even before Daedalus looked, he knew what he would see there: a small, glowing green orb that hovered right above his skin.

It had worked.

He'd never done this spell before—he'd found the form in an ancient text at the Oxford library in England. It had been mistranslated from old Persian, and Daedalus had hired a modern scholar to retranslate it. His hunch had paid off. As far as he knew, no one had manifested a locator orb before, not in centuries.

"Go," he whispered. "Find the circle of ashes."

Fifteen minutes later, it did.

Once again Daedalus stood inside the charred circle that was such a visceral reminder of that night so long ago. The night of creation and destruction.

Now he had a full Treize, the circle, the rite. He was ready at last, after centuries of waiting.

His goal had been achieved, but he knew that others had helped him get here. Jules through the years, Axelle, others. And lately, someone unseen had helped him. Someone who would possibly rejoin the Treize, rendering one of the twins superfluous.

The Endless Cycle

By the time Petra got to Richard and Luc's apartment, she was nursing a deep, smoldering rage.

Richard answered the door, wearing ragged jeans too big for him and an unbuttoned, faded denim shirt.

"Hi," he began, but Petra stepped forward and slapped him across the face as hard as she could. He staggered backward, taken completely off guard, and almost fell against the hallway wall.

"Are you *nuts*?" he exclaimed, one hand over his cheek. He straightened quickly, but not before Petra hauled off and smashed her fist into his ribs. "Ow! Stop it, you crazy old bat!"

Now totally alert, Richard danced away from her.

"I'm going to skin you!" Petra hissed, advancing on him. "And then I'll sew you back into it! You lying *bastard*! You son of a *bitch*! You murdering monster!" Belatedly, Petra had the fervent hope that Clio's vision hadn't been wrong.

"Uh, *what*?" He sounded incredulous, staring at her, still with his hand to his face.

"The twins' spell finally worked," Petra spit out, trying to corner him. "They *saw* you, you bastard! *Saw* you watching the streetcar, summoning the wasps, blowing up Clio's car! It was *you* all along! You tried to kill *Clio!* Clio is my child! I raised her! And Thais, an innocent! They're *my* family! And you stood there and *lied* to me, said they were safe! Said you wouldn't hurt them! You're lucky I don't strike you down where you stand!" She raised one hand in the air, as if to call down a spell that would split him in half.

Richard backed away and held up both hands, ready to ward her off. "I didn't blow up Clio's car," he said quickly. "What are you talking about?"

"Oh, good, look concerned," Petra sneered. "Last night Clio's car exploded. Congrats. Your spell worked. But you must know that."

"Her car explo—is she okay?"

"You do surprised concern very well." Petra's voice sounded like acid dripping. "You missed your calling—you should have gone onstage."

"Is she all right?" Richard's face was stony.

"I'm sure it's a disappointment for you."

Richard stepped forward and grabbed both of Petra's arms, his grip biting into her. "Is. She. All. Right?"

Petra looked at him. This was weird, even for a murderous, lying son of a bitch. "She jumped out a split second before the whole thing went up in flames."

He released her and stepped back, rubbing his

fingers across his forehead. "So she's okay. And it wasn't an accident?"

"What are you playing at?" Petra exclaimed. "Of course it wasn't a bloody accident! You know it wasn't!"

"I didn't do it," he said strongly, looking at her.

"They *saw* you," Petra said. "The twins did a spell, and they saw you do those things."

"They didn't see me blow up the car because it wasn't me."

"You're saying you didn't almost impale Thais on a light pole, didn't summon the wasps, didn't send a guy to mug Clio?" Going through the litany made her anger burn again.

"I'm saying I didn't blow up Clio's car yesterday."

Petra looked at him, at the tight line of his body, his shuttered face, the tattoo she could see on his chest. She shook her head. "You've lost me. You didn't blow up the car, but you did the other things?"

He frowned and moved away from her, walking down the hallway to the kitchen. His tan feet were bare and made no sound on the wooden floor. She followed him.

"If I'd brought my *athème*, I would be cutting out your liver now."

He shot her a glance as he filled a dish towel with ice. "You've become unexpectedly bloodthirsty in your old age, Petra." He held the towel to his cheek, wincing slightly. "Bloodthirsty and weirdly strong." He moved to a cupboard and got down a glass. There was a new bottle of scotch on top of the fridge, and he filled the tumbler half full. "I'd offer you some, but—"

"I'd only spit it in your face." There was something off here, but Petra couldn't put her finger on it.

Richard took a swallow of the liquor, not even wincing when it went down. "I didn't have anything to do with happened to Clio's car. But I did the other things."

Deep down, Petra had hoped that somehow the girls were wrong, that Richard hadn't been behind the attacks. He'd always been in her heart, from the time he was a boy. She'd felt his pain over Cerise and knew what a bad deal he'd gotten out of the rite. For him to have done this—it broke her heart.

"You did the other things." Her knees felt weak and she sat abruptly on an aluminum kitchen chair.

Richard pulled out another chair and sat down across from her. "I did those things before I knew the twins. I wanted them dead."

"In the name of the goddess, *why?*"

He stared into the bottom of his glass. "When Daedalus called me here, I didn't know what was going on. Then he told me about the twins. I knew you'd had Clio—I saw her when she was just a little kid. But twins—as soon as I knew there were two, I wanted to get rid of them."

"You didn't want a full Treize."

"Hell no, I didn't want a full Treize! Why would I? So some other horror could take place? What would it be this time?"

"You think the rite would be worse than your

killing innocent children?" Petra didn't drink—maybe a sip or two of wine every once in a great while. But she would have welcomed a sherry right then. She let out a heavy sigh, feeling tired and discouraged. "Why didn't you come talk to me?"

Richard scoffed. "Yeah. 'Hey, Petra, is it okay if I off those kids?'"

"I could have helped you come up with another way. I thought you wanted to do the rite."

He made an impatient gesture. "I don't need more power—I don't use what I have. Maybe if the rite would make me age naturally or die, then I might go for it. But it's just going to be Daedalus's power grab."

Petra sat and thought for several minutes. Something else was going on, something he wasn't telling her. "Or is it because the twins look so much like Cerise?"

His dark eyes flicked up to meet hers. "Oh, do they?" he said woodenly.

"Is seeing them painful for you? Are you still angry at Cerise for not choosing you?"

"Cerise did choose me," Richard said, and drained his glass. "Yes, Thais and Clio look like Cerise, eerily like. But once I got to know them . . . they don't actually remind me of her very much at all. They're . . . really different."

"Yes, they are." Petra twined her hands together. "What do you mean, Cerise chose you? You said the same thing the other day, that she hadn't rejected you. What are you talking about? Everyone knew

Marcel was with her, and she got pregnant, for God's sake! You couldn't have courted her, not really. You were too—young."

Pain flashed across his face but was gone in an instant. When he looked up again, he had that oddly knowing, adult expression that he'd had even at fifteen, more than two hundred years ago.

"I wasn't too young," he said. "I was too young to marry her, couldn't support her. But I wasn't too young to have her, and I wasn't too young to get her pregnant. Cerise's baby was mine."

"No." Petra frowned, thinking back.

"Yes. It's true that she was with Marcel," he went on, his face twisting with bitterness. "But she'd been lying with me for six months before. She was already pregnant when she was first with him." He got up quickly and poured himself more scotch. Petra wanted to take it from him and give him something else but knew better than to try.

"It was your child?" Petra was awash with emotions, memories, old pain, healed wounds. "You're—quite sure?"

He laughed bitterly. "Oh, yeah."

"Then what was she doing with Marcel? He hoped to marry her!"

Shrugging, Richard sat down again, pulling his shirt closed around him as if cold. "I don't know. I thought I'd die when I found out. She just scolded me for being jealous. Maybe she felt sorry for him. Maybe she wanted to thank him for everything he was doing for you all, your family. After Armand left.

Maybe she really cared about him. I don't know."

"Both of you." Petra shook her head. How much she hadn't known about her daughters. Had she been blind? Stupid? Or just too wrapped up in her own unhappiness and disappointment to see what was happening in front of her nose?

"Yeah. Both of us. Never at the same time, though."

Petra winced.

"Sorry." He shook his head. "She was your daughter, and she was a good daughter. But goddess, it was hard, loving her. Knowing it was my child she carried and her still dallying with that stiff, stuck-up fool—and then she died. And I couldn't even claim the baby."

"Why didn't Marcel?"

"He knew I would kill him if he tried." Richard gave a little smile and drank.

"So he thought the child was yours?"

"I think he hoped it wasn't. He knew I was in the picture, though. Cerise never kept either of us secret from the other."

Standing up, Petra went to get a glass and filled it with tap water. She leaned against the sink and looked at him, feeling overwhelmed by everything she had just learned. So Richard was actually related to Clio and Thais. Very, very distantly—a connection that would barely be acknowledged by a regular person alive today who learned of an ancestor who'd lived and died several centuries ago. But still, there was a thin sliver of connection there. She'd have to take some time to sit with that, consider when it was appropriate to tell the girls. Right now, she knew it was more than they could handle.

"And how does this tie in to the twins?" she asked him.

Richard sighed and rested his head in his hands. It was several minutes before he spoke. "After the rite, we all split apart immediately. Melita disappeared that night and Marcel within days. All of us split away from the *ville*, and my daughter went to live with the Dedouards. I planned to get back to the village when she was old enough to take with me. *But then I didn't age.* I didn't become a grown-up, on the outside, at least. So I only kept tabs on her from a distance. I kept in touch with some people, and they let me know how Hélène was. I watched her grow up from a distance. Grow up and get married and get pregnant and die."

Petra nodded sadly.

"They always die," Richard said.

Petra could tell he was trying to sound cold and distant.

"Daughter after daughter of that line—they always die. I just . . . want it to stop."

She could barely hear his voice.

"If the twins died now, they wouldn't give birth, and that line would end," Petra said. "Is that what you mean? We'd never have to feel the pain of another daughter dying."

His nod was barely imperceptible, and he drained his second glass. An ordinary man would have had no liver left by now.

"And you were willing to commit murder for that."

"I didn't know them. I freaked about Daedalus wanting to do the rite. I don't know—it was like I went crazy for a while. But . . . also, I couldn't follow through. I mean, I'm not Daedalus, but I know my way around a spell. If I'd really, truly wanted them dead at my core, they'd be dead. My spells always had an out."

Petra glared at him. "And that makes it okay?"

"Petra." He gave a bitter laugh and shook his head. "Of course not. It will never be okay. Nothing will ever be okay for any of us ever again. But bottom line, I didn't kill the twins. And I quit trying after the wasps."

"What about my house catching on fire?"

"Wasn't me."

"Clio's car didn't just explode on its own."

"I didn't do it. Petra, I know them now. They're . . . nice kids. I truly regret trying to harm them, and I stopped as soon as it got through to me that they were . . . real. I'm sorry."

"I can't ever trust you again."

Richard looked sad. "I was never that trustworthy to begin with."

"No—you were unreliable, but I did trust you. I trusted you not to hurt me or the people I love."

He was silent for a minute. "If you feel they're still under attack, then you need to figure out who's behind it, and fast. Amazingly, there are people who are even more ruthless than I am."

She looked at him. "If I find out you're lying now, if I find out that you're still trying to hurt those girls . . ."

"You'll cut out my liver with your *athème*, skin me alive and sew me back into it, and what . . . oh, spit scotch in my face. Got it."

"I will make you pay for the rest of your life," she said, getting up. "And, as you're all too aware, that will be a very, very long time."

She left without looking back. Her heart felt heavy with emotion. As relieved as she was to know that Richard was no longer trying to hurt Thais and Clio, that meant that there was still an unknown threat to their lives.

Thais

"Are you sure you don't want a ride?" Kevin asked me on Monday afternoon. He pointed to his car and looked hopeful.

"I would love one," I said. "But I can't. Maybe tomorrow?"

"Tomorrow," Kevin said. He came closer and put his hand on my shoulder, and I felt a comfortable excitement at his touch. "Can I call you later?"

"Of course," I said, and we kissed for just a moment, breaking away before the inevitable catcalls and teasing started. Kevin got in his car and I headed for the streetcar stop.

Petra had put yet more layers of protective spells over me and Clio this morning before school. Last night she'd told us that Richard had confessed to everything up until the wasps but that he swore he wasn't responsible for the house fire or Clio's car. Petra had believed him. Which meant we still had an unknown enemy.

Clio had been hoping that Petra wouldn't even let us go to school today, but she had—Clio told me Petra had always worried that if Clio missed too much school, social services would try to take her away. So Petra had given us a ride here this morning. I'd half expected her to be waiting for us after school, but I hadn't seen her car.

Which was just as well, because I had no intention of going home right away. Apparently neither did Clio, because she'd left with Racey and said she'd see me later.

The streetcar heading downtown came within a few minutes, and a crowd of students got on. I sat on a wooden seat, remembering the light-pole incident. Richard. It was unbelievable—sure, he seemed mysterious and kind of hard, but trying to kill us? I remembered the first few times I'd met him, how cold and weird he'd been. But the more I'd seen him, the more okay he'd seemed, and I'd been starting to like him as a friend. Petra had said that he had been determined for the rite not to happen and that he'd lost his head. He'd tried to hurt us before he'd gotten to know us, and now that he did, there was no way he could do anything to us.

It just went to show, you never really knew anyone. Everyone lied, or left stuff out, or distorted things—especially everyone in the Treize. Even in my own family. Petra had lied to Clio about our dad, and me, and about the fact that she wasn't even Clio's grandmother but just some super-distant relative. Axelle had lied to get me to come live with her. Even Clio had probably lied to me at some point about something.

But it was time to get some straight answers.

Now I knew that it was Richard who'd been trying to kill us. I knew the whole Treize was here in New Orleans. I knew that Clio and I would play a vital part in the rite—if we agreed to it. Now I needed to know how I had gotten here in the first place.

I got off the streetcar at Canal Street, crossed it, and headed into the French Quarter. It felt like I'd lived in New Orleans a long time. Like every day had a year's worth of emotions packed into it, so it was a lifetime ago that I'd lived in Connecticut and years since I'd lived with Axelle.

I'd never given Axelle her key back, and now I let myself in through the side gate. At the apartment door I put my hand out, flat against the door, and closed my eyes.

I got nothing.

Wait—I concentrated hard and felt myself sink surprisingly quickly into a focused state of awareness where I almost melded with the door, with things around me. Inside the apartment I felt Axelle. But no one else. Good.

Unlocking the door, I opened it into the familiar dim, smoke-filled entryway that led directly into the main room. A moment later, Axelle walked out of her bedroom.

"Who's—Thais? How did you get in?"

I dangled the key from my hand. "I want some answers. And you're going to give them to me."

Axelle paused, looking confused. "Clio?"

I stared at her. "No. You can't tell us apart? I used to live with you!"

"Sorry." Axelle curled up in the black leather armchair, crossing her legs over one overstuffed arm. "I knew it was you. But you seemed different. Just for a second. What's up?" She picked up her old-fashioned silver cigarette case and took a cigarette out, lighting it.

I came into the main room and dropped my backpack on the newspaper-littered floor. Axelle was probably missing her personal maid and cleaning service.

"I told you—I want some answers. Let's start with: did you kill my father?"

Axelle looked startled. "This is out of the blue, isn't it? What's going on?"

"I'm just starting at the beginning. Believe me, we're going to get to more recent stuff." I felt very sure of myself, in control. It was unusual, but it also felt natural, like it had been inside me all the time and now was finally coming out. "Now, about my dad?"

Axelle shook her head briskly, swinging her silky black pageboy like a bell. "No, I didn't kill him. Absolutely not."

"So Daedalus did, then?" I asked with surface calm.

"He told me he didn't."

"Do you think he did?"

Axelle seemed to choose her next words carefully. "I'm not sure. I didn't think so at the time—I believed it was all coincidence. But now I'm not sure. It's possible."

Having my dad die in a freak accident had been the worst thing imaginable. Now, believing that he'd been killed—and I did think that Daedalus had killed him—the pain came rushing back at me with a fresh, razor-edged presence. My dad had been killed so that Daedalus could get to me for his own purposes. My dad had died because of me. In that moment, a small, sharp burning ignited inside me, deep in my chest.

"Okay, then." I took in a long, steady breath, trying to stay calm, to not jump up shrieking and wailing. "Next. What's a dark twin?"

Across the room, Axelle's eyes were as black as her hair, as black as the leather chair. Bottomless. "I haven't heard that phrase in a long time," she said slowly. "I think it's an old wives' tale. Where did you hear it?"

"What is it?"

Shrugging, Axelle said, "Well, it's a myth, really. It's when you have identical twins, one egg that splits apart. Instead of each half getting a mix of light and dark, one twin gets mostly light and one gets mostly dark."

"So one twin is evil?"

"Not necessarily." Axelle thought, tapping one finger against her chin. "It's more like, that twin is more *likely* to go dark. But, I mean, no one really thinks it happens. Not really."

Petra does, I thought. *But which one of us is she worried about?*

"What's Daedalus up to, really? With this rite

and the full Treize? Is he planning for one of us to die?"

"No." Axelle frowned. "I don't think so. It's never sounded like he expects anyone to die. Certainly not you or Clio. He was so thrilled about you two. He needs you both to complete the rite. There's no way he would harm one of you, the way Petra worries."

I was about to ask my last question when someone pounded on the apartment door. My breath stilled in my chest as I recognized those vibrations. Luc. Oh no.

Axelle rose with languid grace and sauntered to the door. She opened it, and I caught a glimpse of Luc's dark shadow, followed by a smaller one. I forced myself back to the cool calm I'd been channeling with Axelle and raised my eyes to meet his.

He wasn't expecting to see me, and something lit for just a moment in his dark blue eyes. I clamped down on any response and knew I'd gotten all the answers out of Axelle that I would get. At least today.

Axelle and someone else came into the room, and the other person gasped. I looked at her—her magenta hair, multi-pierced ears, the wild clothes. This must be Claire, I realized. She stared back at me, her hand over her mouth.

"Yes, they do look alike," Axelle said with dry humor. "I assume you two want a drink?"

"God, yes," Claire said with feeling. "It's pretty freaky."

I grabbed my backpack and stood up.

"I've seen maybe eight of that line," Claire went on, still looking at me. Axelle handed her a martini glass and she took a big sip. What was it with the Treize all being lushes? I wondered. Because they didn't need to worry about killing themselves with alcohol? "They've all had the mark, the fleur-de-lis. But none of them has ever looked so . . . exact. Axelle? Did you ever see one like this?" She gestured at me with her drink.

"I'm standing right here. But go ahead and talk about me. It's okay." I couldn't remember ever being so snippy. I moved past Claire toward the front door, not looking at Luc. I hadn't gone four feet when there was a huge crack of lightning that polarized the room for a moment and then an enormous boom of thunder that actually made my chest flutter.

Then the lights went out.

"Damn it," Axelle muttered. "Let me find a candle."

"I can't believe this still happens all the time," Claire said. "Talk about a third-world country."

I made out the dim outline of the door and headed for it again just as Luc's hand brushed my arm—I was inches from him. That barest touch set off a chain reaction, melting my icy shell. I stiffened, pulled my arm away, and moved past him.

"Where are you going?" His low voice still thrilled me, and I so hated it.

"Home." I opened the door and was blasted with sheets of rain and a bolt of lightning so close that I quickly stepped backward. Shoot. This was going to be so awful, slogging up to Canal Street to catch the streetcar. Well, I could duck into a shop or café and wait till it blew over. Getting me home even later. Petra was going to have a fit.

"Thais, wait till it lessens," Axelle said.

"How can she even stand lightning?" I heard Claire mutter.

"You can't go out in this." I felt Luc's heat behind me. What if I closed my eyes and leaned back, felt his arms come around me? God, I was such a jerk. Very nice, very nice to be thinking this when I had Kevin. I was *awful*—not only stupid, but disloyal.

Ignoring all of them, I stepped right out into it, and rain instantly washed over me, pelting my face and hair, gluing my shirt to me.

"I'll give you a ride." Luc turned to Axelle and Claire. "I'm taking Thais to Petra's. I'll be right back."

"No, you're not," I said, and headed out into the storm, crossing the courtyard as fast as I could and getting to a momentary shelter under the covered driveway to the street. Luc caught up to me and touched my arm, and that motion and the rain and my jumbled thoughts added up to a powerful déjà vu of when he had first kissed me, in our private garden. It sent pain jolting through me like lightning, and I whirled, ready to snap his head off.

"Please," he said gently. He dropped his hands to his sides and looked at me. "I won't touch you again. I won't even talk to you if you want. But let me give you a ride home. My car is right there." He pointed through the wrought-iron gate at the street. "It's pouring—I can get you home in ten minutes."

I was suddenly so tired of keeping up my guard and my hurt against him. It took so much effort. I pushed my wet bangs out of my eyes, unwilling to think this through. "Fine," I said. "Whatever."

Luc walked quickly to the gate, as if he wanted to get me in his car before I came to my senses. He went ahead of me to unlock the passenger door for me—what a gentleman—and I followed him.

Jump!

Some sixth sense shouted that at me and I obeyed instantly, leaping sideways, pushing Luc ahead of me. A split second later a heavy metal planter plummeted down from the balcony above us, scraping my arm, and crashed onto the curb, spewing plants and dirt everywhere.

I stared at the planter. It must have weighed sixty pounds at least and would have cracked my head open if it had hit me. Luc and I were semi-sprawled across the hood of the car in back of us. His arms were around me, his face shocked, and he looked up at the balcony where the broken, twisted metal supports dangled from the balcony railing.

"Holy mother!" Luc exclaimed. "Are you all right?"

"Uh . . ." A dim stinging feeling made me look at my arm.

"My arm is scratched."

Luc pulled me farther into the street, standing

next to me in the pouring rain, and looked up at the balcony. "That whole section is rusted through," he said. "It's amazing it hasn't fallen before. Let me see your arm."

"It's just a scratch," I said, not wanting him to touch me. Adrenaline made me even shakier. I felt unsure of myself and just wanted to get home. "Well, I guess it wasn't Richard, this time, anyway."

Luc's eyes narrowed. His face went still and cold. "What do you mean, not Richard?"

Racey gave me a ride downtown after I promised that Nan wouldn't turn her into a toad for aiding and abetting me.

"If she gives me a hard time, I'm going to take it out on you," Racey promised.

"Fair enough."

I had her drop me a couple of blocks from Richard's so I'd have a few minutes to get a grip. Ever since Thais and I had recovered from almost drowning, I'd been dying to get my hands on Richard—in an entirely different way from before. I was still reeling from our discovery. Inside I felt charred, hollowed out by betrayal and disappointment. Out of the fifty guys I'd ever dated, I'd cared about only Luc. Since Luc, the only guy who'd gotten to me at all was Richard. Both were disasters. It made me feel like I wasn't even myself. Things like this didn't happen to fabulous Clio, the envy of most of the girls at my school.

At Richard's, I leaned on the doorbell. I didn't try to see if Luc was there—I didn't care if he was. I was going to tear into Richard no matter what.

Overhead, a bank of dark purple clouds was rolling in fast. We were in for a storm.

No one answered. I forced my breathing to slow, forced my chaotic emotions to quiet. I leaned against the wooden door, resting my forehead against it. Richard was inside, but his presence felt subdued. Maybe he was sleeping.

In our religion, we have several really important rules. The threefold law, for example, where you acknowledge that anything you do, anything you send out into the world, comes back at you three times over. So heads up, basically. And there were other rules about not controlling people, not manipulating events that affect other people, not subverting others' will—I had broken that rule and was walking a dangerous line with it.

Another rule is about not using magick to invade other people—themselves, their thoughts, their space, their things. Not without permission. I was about to do that.

Glancing around first, I traced several signs around the lock on Richard and Luc's front door. I focused, seeing the lock's mechanism inside my head, seeing the tumblers gently shift and fall, and then the lock opened with a gentle click. I turned the doorknob and burst in, slamming the door behind me as hard as I could.

I was halfway down the hall when Richard came out of his room, wary concern on his face. When he saw it was me, his shoulders fell with resignation.

"I know why you're he—" he began as I swung

my heavy messenger bag with all my might. It caught him squarely on his side, knocking him over into the wall of the hallway.

"God da—" he began again, holding up his arm, but I was swinging my other fist. He grabbed it, holding my wrist in a manacle grip, and yanked the messenger bag away. He grabbed my other wrist and I was horrified by how strong he was, how quickly I'd been thwarted. I had pictured him taking my wrath, apologizing, groveling, letting me get my rage out—like most guys did.

I drew back one foot to kick him, but in a second he had hooked his ankle behind mine and pulled, so that I fell heavily to the hard floor. He fell on top of me since he was holding my hands, and my breath whooshed out, leaving me gasping. Quickly he rolled off me so we were side by side, and he got as far away from me as he could before I could knee him where it hurts.

I sucked in a deep breath and started yelling at him. Every bad name, every swearword in English and French that I knew, every hateful thought I'd had about him in the last thirty hours, every ounce of rage and hurt and venom I'd been bottling up since yesterday, I let it all out. My whole life, if anyone had crossed me, from kindergarten to this year, they'd known about it and I'd made them wish they'd never been born. All of those times rolled together wasn't a tenth of what I spewed at Richard now.

Toward the end of my tirade there was a huge

flash of light, as if God had just taken a picture of the world, and then an explosion of thunder that vibrated the floorboards beneath me. The apartment went dark. I struggled as hard as I could, but he held my wrists like iron, until I had angry red marks from his fingers.

Heavy rain pelted the windows in the other room, and more lightning flashed and thunder boomed. I paused to take a breath, and he quickly said, "I was going to come see you and Thais today. I know you're pissed, and I don't blame you. But I can explain."

"Save it!" I spat, trying to jerk my hands free. "You effing bastard! I *hate* you!"

"No, you don't," he said.

"Okay, then, I *despise* you! I *loathe* you! I spit on the ground you walk on!"

In the dim light, Richard's dark eyebrows raised, and then I saw him bite the inside of his cheek, like he was trying not to laugh.

I stared at him. "Don't you dare laugh, you fricking *jerk!*"

He went solemn immediately, shaking his head. "No, no, I'm sorry. I'm not laughing. You've got every right to be furious. It's all my fault. I just—was crazy. I can't explain it. But then I met you, and . . ." He looked down at me, and I caught my breath, remembering another time he had looked down at me. "And I knew I couldn't hurt you." He cleared his throat. "Couldn't bear to see you hurt." His voice was husky now, and because I'm completely *insane*, I became aware of his hard body, pressed against me.

"Even though you're stuck-up," he went on, unbelievably.

My eyes snapped wide open.

"And have had your own way far too much," he went on, "and are spoiled and have Petra wrapped around your little finger, and are way too beautiful for your own good, and are used to stupid little boys hanging on your every word, and—"

His words were drowned out by my outraged screech, and I bucked hard, trying to break his grip. Then he was smiling down at me, as if he thought I were fabulous, and, goddess help me, he was beautiful, in a weird, young way, completely unlike Luc.

"Don't you look at me like that," I hissed. "You tried to *kill* me and my sister! And then you made out with me! When I think about it, I want to throw up!" Abruptly my throat closed and I felt my nose twitch with impending tears.

Richard was solemn again. "I don't want to hurt you," he said quietly in the darkness. "I only kissed you after I had given up the whole plan. And last time, *you* grabbed *me*."

"Don't remind me," I snapped. "I'm so ashamed, I don't know if I'll ever live it down!"

He drew back then, and I was amazed to see that he looked hurt.

"Well, it'll be our secret," he said evenly.

That deflated me. I slumped against the floor, away from him, trying to figure things out. Richard was very still and quiet, his face the same cool mask as when I'd met him. I hadn't realized how much emotion he'd been showing me, how much his guard had been down, until I saw him again like this.

I wriggled my hands tiredly. "Let me go."

He did, releasing my wrists. I looked at them, the dark red marks, and knew I'd have bruises tomorrow. I rubbed my wrists with my hands, easing the ache, and just lay on the hard wooden floor, my back to him. Clio the Magnificent, as some guy had called me in tenth grade. *Look at me now,* I thought dully. *I'm a freaking waste of space. Like a crumpled pile of dirty clothes, lying here on the floor.*

"Why did you do it?" I asked finally. "Why did you want to hurt me—us?" I hated how small and vulnerable I sounded.

"Didn't Petra tell you?" he asked. His expression changed suddenly as something seemed to occur to him. "What did she tell you, exactly, about our conversation?"

I frowned. "She said that you went crazy or something, that you just wanted all this stuff to end, and it seemed like the way to make it stop was to get one of us out of the picture. But I still don't get it; I don't get how you could have done those things to us."

Richard winced. "I'm sorry," he said. "Truly." He paused. "Did Petra say—anything else? About . . . my connection to you and Thais?"

What was he getting at? "She said . . . once you knew us, you stopped." I thought for a second. It

200

seemed like there was something else, something he was rooting for in my mind, the way he stared at me so intently. "Nan said we looked like Cerise. I hadn't realized that," I remembered. The next question was obvious—*Was that why you wanted me?*—but I didn't want to know the answer.

"You're not anything like her," Richard said.

"What?" I closed my eyes, feeling like I couldn't get up. It was dark, and the rain and thunder and lightning were soothing, so much bigger than my pathetic life. I wanted to be in a cocoon of gray light and rain.

"Cerise. You're not anything like her. You don't remind me of her. You don't even look like her, really. Just a superficial resemblance."

"We look exactly like her," I said in a monotone. "People gasp when they see us." *And that's the only reason you ever came after me.* I remembered Marcel's reaction and realized why it had been so strong. Had Thais told me we looked like Cerise? I didn't remember.

"They're not seeing you. Cerise was . . . light, like honey. Like sunlight. Easy to hold but impossible to keep. Like a butterfly."

"Not like me." It seemed like one more damning thing against me.

"No." Richard gave a short laugh. "You're not a butterfly. You're not light or easy."

There was silence between us for some time.

"You're not honey," Richard finally went on. "You're wine. You're the deepest, darkest shadow under a tree on a blazing day. You're strong and hard, coursing like a current at the bottom of a river."

I started crying silently, my tears running across my face to drip to the floor.

"I don't love anybody." Richard's voice was bleak. "I don't love you. But I see the value of you, the incredible worth of you—I see more in you than in anyone I've ever known. I am so sorry for what I did, and I would *never* hurt you now that I know you."

We were there like that for a while, with me weeping silently and Richard not touching me. I wished someone could hold me. Eventually I stopped crying. Finally, feeling like I was a thousand years old, much older than *him*, I sat up. I had the thought that if I felt like this now, immortality was going to be harder than I imagined.

"I have to go." I got to my feet awkwardly. My wrists burned.

"Clio—believe that I'm so sorry about how I tried to hurt you and Thais. I can't really explain it, except I just went crazy. But you have to know that I would *never* hurt you now. I wouldn't let anyone else hurt you if I knew about it. When Petra told me about your car catching on fire, I was—"

I picked up my purse and my messenger bag and brushed dust off my clothes. Not looking at him, I headed to the front door, knowing I must look like I'd been dragged through a hedge backward. Whatever.

His warm hand touched my upper arm, holding it lightly, keeping me there. "Clio."

"Don't touch me."

He let go at once, and I walked to the door. It was going to be a long, wet walk to Canal Street.

As I reached the front door, I realized that someone was talking loudly outside, and then the door flew open and Luc was there, right in my face.

"Where is he?" Luc said, his eyes cold and hard.

"Luc, come *on*," said Thais, and I saw her right behind him.

"What's going on?" I asked as Luc pushed past me.

"You bastard!" Luc shouted, lunging for Richard, who already looked beaten down and weary. Luc slammed his hands against Richard's shoulders, shoving him into the wall—I heard Richard's head crack against it, saw him wince.

But not fight back.

"What were you thinking?" Luc yelled. "What were you doing? Have you finally gone totally insane? Clio and Thais!" He pushed Richard hard again, and Richard staggered but stayed on his feet.

"Get in line, Thais," Richard said over Luc's shoulder. "First Petra, then Clio, then Luc, then you. And I guess Ouida and Sophie and whoever else gives a crap will show up soon."

"How could you do it?" Luc shouted again. "How could you try to *kill* them? Are you a *murderer*? How could you possibly stand to hurt them?"

Richard frowned, straightening up. "I don't know," he said. "You tell me."

Luc's face flushed, his hands curled into fists.

"I mean, how could I *possibly* do something stupid and boneheaded that would hurt the twins when I don't even know them?" Richard's voice was mocking and sardonic.

"Shut up! I didn't try to *kill* them."

"No. But I wonder who hurt them more?"

They stood there glaring at each other, both tense, ready to spring.

I looked at Thais, the only person I was happy to see in this whole mess. I would worry about what she was doing with Luc later. Right now, she was my sister and the only person in the room I didn't want to shred.

"I'm sick of both of them," I told her. "Let's split."

"Oh God, yes," Thais said, holding the door open.

Then we were out in the rain, walking toward Canal Street. The rain actually felt good, and I knew I couldn't possibly look worse.

"So," said Thais after a couple of blocks. "You gave Richard a hard time?"

"Yeah. It was pretty ugly." I shifted my bag to my other shoulder. "What were you doing with Luc?"

"I went to Axelle's to wring some answers out of her." Thais sounded as fed up and tired as I felt. "Luc was there, and he followed me out of Axelle's when I left, and then we almost got plantered to death."

"What?"

She told me about how a huge, heavy planter had narrowly missed her. A long scratch on her arm looked red and painful.

"Was this another attack, or was it a coincidence?" I asked, knowing that there weren't any coincidences.

"I don't know," Thais said. "It looked all rusty, like it might have happened anytime. Anyway, I was freaked, and I said something like, I guess it wasn't Richard this time. And then Luc ran with it from there."

"Well, maybe they'll kill each other," I said hopefully.

Thais looked at me, and a smile turned up the corners of her mouth. Suddenly it felt okay to smile myself, and we grinned at each other. Sisters.

Tonight

Petra finally saw Clio and Thais on a streetcar, with rain running down the window next to them. They looked alive, if not well, and Petra couldn't see or feel any sense of dark intent around them.

The crystal icicle she was scrying in was still spinning in the window when she realized that someone was knocking on the front door.

Daedalus.

Wonderful. This would be the crowning touch to an already tense, frustrating day.

Petra opened the door, and as soon as she saw his exultant face, she realized that the time she'd been dreading was at hand.

"We have everything," he announced, stepping across her threshold as if walking onto a stage. "The final form of the rite is complete. We have a full Treize. And I have found the Circle of Ashes."

With long practice Petra kept the dismay off her face. He'd found the Circle of Ashes? They should have cloaked it better.

"The time is now," Daedalus said grandly.

"Now? You mean, before Monvoile?"

"I mean now, tonight," Daedalus said.

"Tonight!"

"Yes. Everything is aligned, as if it were all decreed by the heavens." Daedalus smoothed his hair back with one hand.

What a load of . . . hot air, Petra thought.

"Please get Clio and Thais and meet us at the circle at midnight tonight." Daedalus handed her a printout of a map and directions. He didn't know that she, Ouida, and Sophie had found the circle weeks ago. "The rite will begin at precisely twelve twenty-seven, when the moon is at its utmost fullness."

"I don't think we're ready to do the rite," Petra tried.

"You will be." Daedalus looked down at her, and then his face softened. Unexpectedly, he took one of her hands in both of his. "Petra. We've had more than two hundred years to think about this, to dream about it. To prepare for it. On that terrible night so long ago, Melita gave us all a gift and a curse. This is our chance to heal past injuries, to enhance our gifts, correct our curse, and achieve that which is dearest to our hearts. You're ready for it. You've been ready for it for a long, long time."

She looked directly at him. "I don't trust you."

He laughed, putting his head back. Petra remembered that he had been handsome as a young man. But he hadn't aged well. Instead of achieving distinction, he had acquired only superciliousness.

"The beauty is, you won't need to, my dear," he

said. "Each of us brings to the rite our own strengths, our own powers. None of us is a Melita. Each of us may have different goals. We might not agree with or support each other's goals—they're inherently personal, relating only to ourselves. Take care of yourself, and everything will be well."

He let go of her hand and walked to the front door. "At midnight, then." His eyes were sparkling, his face animated and alive. Still smiling, he let himself out, not seeming to mind that Petra hadn't promised to come.

She hadn't expected things to happen this quickly. There were arrangements she still had to make. But at least the important plans were already in place, the key individuals ready to fulfill their roles. It was a shame, the price it would cost, but at least it was a cost another was already looking to pay.

The rain had stopped. Petra was in the newly replanted front garden when she felt the girls walking home from the streetcar stop. They had deliberately disobeyed her, completely flouted her authority, and, what's more, hadn't been stopped by the knowledge that she would be out of her mind with worry.

They paused at the front gate, seeing her kneeling on the damp brick walk next to the small bed of herbs.

"Nan," Clio said.

Petra looked up. They both looked like drowned rats, almost as bad as when she'd pulled them out of the waterspout—oh goddess, had that been only *yesterday*? But looking more closely at Clio, Petra saw that she had been crying and looked shaken and upset. She'd gone to see Richard, Petra assumed immediately. But surely he hadn't put those bruises on her wrists? Not unless he'd lost his mind for good this time.

"Um, hi, Petra," said Thais.

"You're both really wet. Go inside and change your clothes. I'll put the kettle on to make tea. Then we need to talk."

Thaïs

Half an hour later the three of us sat around the kitchen table, mugs of hot tea in front of us. "If you believe that Richard didn't blow up Clio's car, then who's doing it?" I asked. "I mean, maybe the planter wasn't an attack, but maybe it was. It has to be one of the Treize."

"Yes, I think you're right," Petra said, frowning. "I truly don't know who, though. However, I think it will all probably come to a head tonight." Her clear blue-gray eyes met mine and then Clio's across the table. "Daedalus stopped by. He wants to do the rite tonight, at midnight."

My heart seemed to seize in my chest. We'd been dancing around this idea for weeks now, almost pretending it wasn't real, wasn't coming. Now Petra was saying that it was coming right at us, right now.

"Tonight?" Clio said, looking alarmed. "But I'm not ready. I mean, we're not ready, none of us. Right?"

Petra sighed. "I'm about as ready as I'll ever be. I've put certain plans in place for the rite. I know you two will be safe. I don't know what else will happen."

"That's just it!" I exclaimed. "No one does. Everyone seems to think something different will happen. But I've got no idea what it will do to *me*. Plus, the last time we did a circle with Daedalus, he used our power without permission."

"I've thought about that," Petra said. "But Ouida, Sophie, and some others are all in agreement. I'm sure that neither of you will be harmed tonight. Nor can Daedalus take anyone's power unless they give it to him."

I took a sip of tea, my mind whirling. "This is all happening much too fast." I thought about Clio and how she was studying Hermann Parfitte's book.

"Couldn't we wait a couple of weeks?" Clio asked, as if she had read my mind.

Petra looked at her. "Why? I don't think it will make any difference to you two."

Clio and I met eyes, and I knew she wanted more time to work on her spells. But she wouldn't tell Petra that.

"Tonight is when a lot of different elements come together," Petra explained. "The phase of the moon, the position of the stars, the time of the year—apparently it's all just right, perfect for the rite to happen tonight."

"But what's going to *happen?*" I asked pointedly. "What will happen to *us?*"

"I think you'll get a huge surge of power," Petra said. "After the rite, I believe your magick will be much stronger, though neither of you has gone through your rite of ascension."

"What else?" After Récolte, I'd felt terrible.

"I don't think you're going to become immortal," said Petra. "Is that what you're worried about?"

"Among other things." I couldn't believe this conversation was part of my life. "I thought I would have a lot more time to think about this. Why don't you think we'll become immortal?"

"No one will be spelling you to be." Petra looked into her tea mug, as if the answers lay there. "I'll be spelling you to be protected, to be safe. But no one will be trying to make you immortal."

Clio looked disappointed, but then her face became determined, which gave me a bad feeling.

"Can we refuse to go?"

Petra looked thoughtful. "We could, of course, but actually, honey, I don't think it would make much difference. There are reasons to do the rite—to become more powerful, more in tune with magick. To help our friends if we can. To learn. Because I'm sure you won't be harmed, it seems pointless to refuse to go."

I didn't know what to think. I'd been hoping that if enough time went by, I could ride out Clio's plan to become immortal. Maybe with time I'd feel more prepared, more braced. Now it was happening much too fast. I was somewhat reassured by Petra's promise of safety and the knowledge that no one could spell us to be immortal. But I was worried about what Clio was thinking, what she might be planning to do.

Q-Tip jumped up on the kitchen table, rubbing against Petra's arm.

"Hi, baby," Clio said gently, reaching out to pet him. He shied away from her, hurrying across the table and jumping off next to me. Clio gazed after him, looking upset.

I got up and put my mug in the sink. "I'm going to take a hot bath."

"Good idea," said Petra. "Put some rose petals and lavender in the water and relax."

That didn't seem too likely.

Upstairs I got my robe and was heading into the bathroom when Clio appeared at the top of the stairs.

"Can you come into my room for a sec?" she whispered.

In her room I sat down on her bed, the only clear surface. She shut the door and sat next to me.

"I don't want to do the freaking rite," I said.

Clio nodded. "I need more time to get ready. But still—if we have to do it tonight, I feel like it will be okay. I do know how to protect from Daedalus taking our power. And Nan's covering the other bases."

I shook my head, not convinced.

"I do," she insisted. "I won't be trying to get anyone else's power. All I'd be doing is protecting us."

I put my head in my hands. "You can't make us immortal?"

"I don't think so," she said regretfully. "Maybe in another month . . ."

"I'm just . . . afraid."

"So am I," Clio surprised me by saying. "I've never been part of anything like this. I mean, you know—things like this just don't happen. Not anymore. Not that anyone would hear about, anyway." She leaned back against the wall, her legs straight out. "This is some freaky stuff, Thais. But . . . I believe Nan. I believe that she'll make sure we're safe. She may have lied about a lot, but she's always protected me. I know since you've discovered magick, you've seen it get all wonky pretty easily. But remember, this is different—these are people who've spent all this time working on their powers. And I can protect us too, guard against our power being used. I mean, isn't it kind of exciting in a way? Tonight is the culmination of hundreds of years of history."

"Tonight is why they killed my dad. Our dad."

Clio's face went white. "What?"

"I talked to Axelle. I'm pretty sure Daedalus killed him to get me here," I explained. "So how can I do this? Just on principle, I hate everything about it, don't want any part of it. It would be like justifying what they did." My poor dad. From the time he'd met our mom, he'd stumbled from one lie to another. That she was a witch. That he'd had two children, not just one. That we could live a normal life if we weren't in Louisiana. And then he'd been killed. What a bad deal he'd gotten, just because he'd fallen in love with our mom. And no one ever talked about her. I had no idea what she'd been like.

"Yeah, I get what you mean," Clio said. "But . . . see, if we do this, but play by our rules—it'll show them that they can't control us like they think they can. We're strong, Thais. We're weirdly strong together. The two of us can show them that they can't mess with us, that we're calling the shots for ourselves, now and for the rest of our lives."

I gazed up at the ceiling, seeing the fine cracks in the old-fashioned plaster.

Clio was silent for a minute, regarding her sparkly purple toes. "It might not even work," she said finally. "Who knows if they've really re-created the rite the way they need to? But as long as we're there for each other, with Petra watching out for us, you and I will be okay. And if we don't go . . . we'll never know who's trying to kill us. They'll just keep trying, and what if it works next time?"

I shivered, already knowing there was no point saying anything else.

We were going to this rite.

Please Forgive Me

Sophie gripped the steering wheel tighter, hoping Manon would assume she was tense because of the rite. Which she was, of course. She and Manon had talked everything out exhaustively, over and over. She felt like she'd been crying for years. But now she knew without a doubt what Manon planned to do.

Next to her, one small hand reassuringly on Sophie's leg, Manon was oddly calm.

Sophie swallowed and peered into the darkness, looking for a road sign. She only hoped that someday Manon would be able to forgive her for what she was about to do.

A Burst of Divine Power

"Are you all right?" Ouida's concerned voice was soothing in the car's darkness.

"Yes, quite. Thank you." Marcel felt more all right than he would have thought possible, thanks to Petra. Now he was quietly exultant, filled with hope and anticipation. At last, at last, his hope and dream, his longing would come true. It would serve Daedalus right.

Had He Learned Nothing?

Petra glanced at the twins in the backseat. Thais looked sad and afraid. Clio looked both calm and expectant . . . which was worrisome. What was on her mind? *Please, goddess, don't let her be planning anything stupid*, Petra prayed silently. Well, Petra would just have to be alert, ready to circumvent it.

Petra was sure Thais was regretting every aspect of her new life, new religion, new relatives. But after tonight, things would settle down some, at least for a while.

It wasn't hard to find the site. Daedalus had written very clear directions, and besides, Petra had been here recently. She turned in to an unmarked, unpaved road; its crushed white shells practically glowed in the bright moonlight. She glanced up at the sky through the windshield. It was perfectly clear, the stars popping brightly.

That would change soon.

Two miles down the road, they were deep in a wooded area, the trees so close on either side of the car that leaves brushed the windows. Then they suddenly gave way into a rough-mown meadow where several other cars were parked. Petra stopped her Volvo next to Ouida's rental and killed the engine. Turning in her seat, she looked back into the solemn identical faces of her descendents, her adopted granddaughters, the people she had chosen to value above all else.

"From here we have to walk a bit," she said, her voice sounding loud in the still night. "Are you guys okay?"

They nodded, and Clio muttered, "Yeah."

Together the three of them walked down the narrow path that led into the blackest, most unlit part of the swamp. The air was cool and damp here, and mosquitoes buzzed all around them.

Behind her, the girls were quiet, trying not to stumble on the uneven ground. They were unusually subdued, despite Petra's promise that they would be safe. It was almost as if they knew what Petra had done: someone had to die tonight for the rite to work.

And Petra knew who it would be.

Clio

After a tense, silent car ride, Petra finally parked and told us to follow her through dense woods. I walked with her and Thais toward the spot where we were meeting the rest of the Treize and almost froze when I realized we had reached the Circle of Ashes, the place Thais and I had seen several times in dreams and visions.

It was creepy and amazing to be standing here, and I was so wound up I could practically feel the earth's energy entering me through the soles of my feet.

I wished I'd had more time to work on my spells. I hadn't gotten far enough in Hermann Parfitte's book to really understand about achieving immortality. But I could at least keep Daedalus from using my power if he tried. Nan would keep us safe from harm; I would keep us from being used.

That awful scene with Richard had replayed itself in my mind twenty times while I got ready for tonight. Again it had struck me how unlike myself I felt lately—weaker, less brash, less bold. And Thais was seeming just the opposite—stronger, more sure of herself.

I blinked as something hit me. That spell we had done to join ourselves. What if it had gone farther than we intended? I frowned, thinking back to the limitations I had put on it. Had I forgotten some aspect of the limitations? Were Thais and I merging or, worse, becoming each other?

I didn't want to be Thais. It was hard enough being Clio.

Maybe it had been the spell. Or maybe I was just turning into a huge crybaby wuss. That was going to stop tonight.

I had taken extra care with my appearance, like old times. My hair was glossy and shiny, parted in the middle, hanging down to frame my face. My makeup was subtle but effective and counteracted the pale, drained, weepy look I'd come home with. I wore solid copper bracelets to cover the bruises on my wrists. For magick like this, no mixed-metal jewelry could be worn.

Finally, I wore the *bouvre* that I'd been saving for my rite of ascension. Tonight seemed important enough for it. It was made of heavy green silk several shades darker than my eyes. The sleeves were long and tight to the elbows, then flared out in bells around my hands. It fitted more closely than most *bouvres* and had embroidery around the waist, like a belt, and around the hem. We would be barefoot, but I wore solid copper anklets.

I looked fabulous. Very much like the old Clio.

"Petra."

A young woman stood next to Jules at the edge of the circle. Her hair was wild, spiky, and dyed pinkish red. Her ears gleamed with lots of silver earrings.

"Hello, Claire," Nan said kindly. They embraced, then Nan introduced us.

"Thaïs I met this afternoon," said Claire, coming to shake my hand. "So this is Clio." She gave me an open, slightly mocking smile, and I realized I liked her right away. She didn't seem as stuffed-shirty as some of the other Treize did.

"Hi," I said. She had green eyes, like we did, but a different shade.

"Welcome, all," I heard Daedalus say, and I turned to see him, arms outstretched, at the opposite edge of the circle. "Thank you so much for coming."

"Your guest speaker will be Father Daedalus," Thaïs murmured in my ear. "Refreshments will be served by the Ladies' Altar Guild."

I stifled a laugh.

"It's now almost midnight," Daedalus went on. "And we're all here."

I hadn't looked around, hadn't looked for Richard or Luc. Now I shook my hair back over my shoulders, chin up, looking calm, cool, and collected. I hoped. I kept my eyes on Daedalus, but it was torture not examining everyone's expression.

"My friends and our two newest members, two

222

hundred and forty-two years ago, we first began this journey together," Daedalus began. And basically he went on like that for ten minutes, droning on about their incredible voyage of discovery that made it all sound like a National Geographic special.

I eased myself behind Nan and surreptitiously looked around, my eyes passing across everyone there. Sophie looked white-faced and tense, Manon calm and unafraid. Ouida and Nan both looked alert. Marcel stood next to Ouida, and he seemed okay, almost excited. Jules was impassive, head lowered, listening to Daedalus. Axelle moved from foot to foot like a racehorse impatient to take off. Claire's expression was outwardly calm, but the tight lines around her brightly painted mouth hinted at more under the surface.

Luc. The one time I glanced at him, he was looking at me. At me, not at Thais. He looked like he wanted to be anywhere but here. Across the circle, opposite Luc, Richard stood, his face hard, his jaw set. He was looking around at everyone, and I thought I saw a glance pass between him and Petra. For a moment his eyes met mine, and I got a jolt of emotion from him, which then immediately shut down. I glanced away, confused. During a circle, if people have a connection, you can pick up feelings from them, but we were just standing here.

"So let us join hands," Daedalus said, "around our ceremonial fire."

One by one we walked into the large circle he had drawn around the charred circle of earth. A small fire blazed in the middle, and four smallish, beat-up wooden cups held the four elements around it. Next to the fire was a slab of white marble, and on the marble was some kind of a stone knife with a carved handle. Daedalus closed the circle around us, and at that moment an unexpectedly cool breeze rustled my hair and brushed against my skin. Clouds had rolled in while Daedalus was speaking, and now every star had been wiped out. The sky was dark purple, and in the distance, I saw clouds lit up by lightning.

Next to me, Thais touched my hand. She'd just noticed the sky. She was trying to keep her fear down, but I could feel it. I was open to everything right now, receiving impressions from everyone and everything around me.

In the circle Ouida came and deliberately put herself between me and Nan, taking my hand in hers. So it was Nan, Ouida, me, Thais, Claire, Richard, Sophie, Jules, Manon, Luc, Daedalus, Axelle, and Marcel next to Nan on her other side. Thirteen of us. A Treize. Someone here was frustrated that Thais and I were alive and here. I couldn't see any sign on anyone's face that told me who it was.

"Let us begin," Daedalus said, and as if on cue, lightning flashed and thunder sounded threateningly. Thais let out a breath, and I squeezed her hand. The circle began moving dalmonde, clockwise, and Daedalus began to sing something that I couldn't understand. I assumed it was in old, old French, just as it had been in 1763, when this rite had first been done. I had a quick thought: myself, two hundred years from now, doing the rite one more time.

Jules began to sing, blending his deep voice smoothly with Daedalus's. Under my breath, I began my own spell, first outlining the limitations, hoping I wasn't leaving anything out, and then weaving the rest of the spell around me and Thais. Again I wished I'd had more time to practice, but the words spun out of my mouth smooth and light and easy. To me that felt like the magick was right. As the circle moved more quickly around the crackling fire, the air around us dropped in temperature and the wind felt cool and damp.

Everyone was singing now. Daedalus's voice was like the main branch of a wisteria vine, with everyone else's voices twining around his. They wove in and out and around each other, each one distinct, yet blending into an almost seamless whole. I caught the words *collet, tâche, plume, cindres*, which I'd heard somewhere before. Holding tightly to Thais's hand, I finished the second section of my spell and began the third.

Nothing startling seemed to be happening, except the magickal energy was rising faster and fuller than I'd ever felt it. The wind kicked up, blowing our hair, our gowns, making leaves swirl in tiny cyclones here and there. The fire cast a pretty, rosy warmth on everyone's faces.

From time to time I closed my eyes so I could concentrate on my own spell. Thais was singing next to me, and I recognized her song. She didn't know Daedalus's spell, of course, so she was simply calling power to her. Our clasped hands felt hot. The ground itself pulsed with energy and power. Wind whipped my hair into my face for a moment, and I accidentally skipped a verse of my spell, only remembering it halfway through. Damn it. I had to begin the third section all over again.

Thais squeezed my hand. Opening my eyes, I saw her worried face.

"Is this a hurricane?" she managed to get out.

Around us, trees waved and bent. The wind was strong and cold and smelled like rain. The clouds above us were churning, lit from within by almost constant lightning.

I shook my head. My heart was pounding. I felt frighteningly full of energy. "Just big magick."

Her face fell, and I wasn't thrilled either. Nan's eyes were closed as she sang strongly, her feet sure on the packed-down grass. The fire's glow glided over her face, softening it, making her look younger.

Quickly I plowed on with my spell, needing to finish it as fast as possible. Everyone was singing loudly, though the wind snatched our voices away, twisting them up into the clouds, spiking them with lightning.

Luc's face was flushed, unbearably handsome,

and my heart ached. Ouida, on my right-hand side, was intent, her smooth brown skin glistening with mist. Manon was joyful, almost skipping to keep up with the circle's speed, her face alight with hope. And Richard . . . was looking at me, his eyes dark and intense. I saw his mouth moving but couldn't distinguish his voice. We didn't love each other, didn't even like each other, and he'd tried again and again to harm me. But I somehow believed that he would never try to hurt me now.

Drawing in a deep breath, I began the last part of my spell.

Lightning struck so close by that I jumped. My hair felt electrified, standing on end. A gray sheet of rain drew over us, soaking us with one sweep. My gown stuck to me uncomfortably as thunder rumbled through my stomach.

My chest felt full and tight, my body so strung with magick that I might burst. I blinked and for just a second was back in my vision, watching the circle do exactly this: the storm, the song, the rite, the rain. Only this time there was no Cerise.

Just her look-alikes.

Fear rushed over me then, huge and terrible and stunning. In one second I couldn't think, couldn't breathe, could hardly move: I was paralyzed with terror, an unnamed, animal-like terror that this was too big, dark, dangerous, deadly, and that I shouldn't be here, I shouldn't be here, I shouldn't be here. . . .

Boom! The world whited out, as though in a

blizzard. The blast of electricity knocked me backward several feet, wrenching my hands away from Ouida's and Thais's. Thunder shook the actual ground like an earthquake, shaking people apart, wrecking the circle. My skin sizzled, and I felt the lightning even before it snaked down from the sky, crisp and thorny and whiter than the sun. It blasted down, blowing a hole in the world where our fire had been. Daedalus, Marcel, Richard, Ouida, and Nan—Sophie and Manon—they each shouted, all different things, all at the same time.

The lightning splintered, whipping into each of us, throwing me to the ground. Daedalus raised his hands in exultation, laughing, feeling the power. In the next moment the lightning jumped, enormous and horrifying. Nan threw her arms out as if to embrace Marcel, and he held his arms open, his face to the sky. Instantly the lightning coalesced, leaving all of us, and speared Marcel in his chest, blowing him off his feet. In its glow I saw Marcel's shock, his face twisting in pain—and then he fell heavily to the ground, dead.

The aftermath was still and quiet. The storm lessened immediately, leaving a stunned vacuum in its wake. The drumming rain became a gentle shower. We all stared at Marcel, who lay faceup, glassy-eyed, on the ground.

"Oh my God," said Claire. "He's dead!" She looked at us all, dumbfounded. "Marcel is dead!"

Thais made a small sound of terror, and I looked at her. She was greenish around the edges and swayed on her feet. I staggered over and caught her as she was going down. Clumsily we both collapsed, just a few feet from Marcel's body.

"What have you done!" Daedalus shouted, his face a mask of fury. "How *dare* you! How *dare* you circumvent the rite!" He shook his fist at Petra, who sank down next to me, looking ill.

"He wanted to die," Petra said weakly. "He wanted to die, and someone had to die for the rite to work. You know that." She met Daedalus's glare. "I had to make sure it wasn't either of my girls. So Marcel and I made a pact."

"How *dare* you!" Daedalus shouted again. "Who helped you? Anyone who helped you will answer to me!" He looked around wildly from face to face.

Sophie was gaping, leaning against a tree. Her long, dark hair streaked down her back. Manon, on her hands and knees, stared at Sophie.

"No one helped me," Petra said, her voice hoarse. "It was just Marcel and me. I'm sorry, Daedalus. I know how much this meant to you. But I couldn't let you kill the one you wanted to."

He opened and closed his mouth several times as members of the Treize turned to look at him.

"And who would that be, Daedalus?" Richard asked quietly.

Daedalus shut his mouth with a snap. "You don't know what you're talking about," he ground out. "I wasn't going to kill anybody! I need everyone here! You've destroyed my life's work! You've

229

destroyed our one chance to have everything we've ever dreamed of!"

"I've destroyed your chance to have everything *you* ever dreamed of," Petra said sadly. "But knowing you, I'm sure you'll create another chance for yourself."

I heard a gasp but couldn't see where it came from. Then a groan.

Claire drew in a breath. "Marcel!"

On the ground, Marcel coughed and groaned again. He blinked several times, then seemed to register that there were trees overhead and that rain was hitting his face.

"Am I not dead?" His voice was a rusty metal whisper.

Luc knelt next to him, his face bitter. "Marcel—you're immortal, man. Get used to it."

Standing, Luc looked at Daedalus, at Petra, at the rest of the Treize. Not at me or Thais. He shook his head, seeming disgusted, then walked off in the rain in the direction of the cars.

"There's no Source," said Jules. He pointed at the charred ground, the jagged hole blasted into the earth. "The Source didn't reappear. This was all for nothing."

"So this is it," Thais said so softly I could hardly hear her. "All of this, the lies, the manipulations, the secrets, the alliances, the research—it was all for nothing."

"Not for nothing, my dear," Petra said, just as softly. "Maybe Daedalus's rite didn't work, but there were many spells being worked here tonight, many people calling on magick for their own uses."

I looked down at my hands, where the bright copper bracelets still rested against Richard's bruises. *Interesting*, I thought. How many other people were working spells, and for what? Had any of them taken?

Had mine?